Delano

John Orozco

ISBN 0-9664816-1-5

Parnassus
Julian CA

This is for my family and friends; their patience and faith have given me the confidence to pursue my dreams. I thank them.

I would also like to thank Mario Roccatani for his vision and his ever demanding attention to detail.

Pursuant to a court order, the pub-
lisher includes the following:

"This book is a pack of lies written
by a disturbed person. Furthermore,
he stole all of the good ones from
my unpublished monograph, *Waltzing With Mannequins*." — W.A.G.

1

My Big Toe

You might think I'm stupid for shooting off my big toe, but at the time it seemed like a good idea.

Even before they sent me to Vietnam, I wasn't entirely convinced that going into combat was good for my country, the Vietnamese people or myself.

Don't misunderstand me; I'm not noble, and I'm not entirely against the army. The army is a good thing for a lot of people who would otherwise be socially out of place because of their homicidal tendencies.

What I was primarily against was that my life and well-being were about to be put at risk for a cause I did not fully appreciate. And to think that this was expected of me while hundreds of thousands of young men my age were having the times of their lives, smoking dope and getting laid in perfectly safe environments.

But don't think that shooting off my toe was some kind of foolish lark. There were serious consequences. First, I could have been court-martialed if my scheme had been discovered, and this would have been an entirely different story. Second, I had to learn how to walk without a big toe on my right foot. My advice to anyone who ever feels the necessity to shoot off his toe is to shoot off a little one. It's probably not as debilitating, and it will serve whatever purpose you have just as well as if you had shot off a big one.

There are probably a lot of people who will think that what I did makes me a selfish coward, but that doesn't necessarily make me a bad person. In fact, selfishness, and what I prefer to call a healthy survival instinct, are exactly what made this country what it is today.

I didn't always see things this clearly, but I've come to terms with myself living in a remote part of Northern California. In fact,

5

I've made what most of my friends would call a phenomenal transformation. Today, in spite of the war, drugs, wicked women and higher education, I'm at long last at peace with the world.

You may ask just how this transformation occurred, and I have every intention of telling you.

It wasn't easy.

I owe part of my self-enlightenment to Winston Ashford Gonzales. Without him, I would have probably ended up married and teaching in a public school. It's not that he simply taught me how to cut corners, though that was part of my success. He taught me a way of seeing and doing things without the excess baggage of guilt.

I don't believe that I was ever one of those guilt-ridden souls who harbored deep resentments. But Winston noticed in me a healthy irreverent quality, and he helped me develop it into its full potential. That was Winston's special skill. He could see through people. He understood their motives immediately. For instance, when he learned of my missing toe, he knew instantly that it had a self-serving motive behind it.

I have to admit there were times when I did not trust him, and I actually felt bad about some of the dishonest things I did. But after sorting it all out, I've forgiven myself. Winston would be proud of me. The only regret I have now is that I didn't know him sooner.

I suppose I should get on with the story and tell you about myself.

I inherited my father's Mexican oval face and high cheekbones. I inherited a strong chin from my mother. I also got her blue-green eyes that seemed out of place with the long, black eyelashes I got from my father. If it were not for an errant baseball, my nose would be perfect. But a girl once told me I was lucky it was hooked and skewed, or I would be pretty.

I always tried to simplify my life as much as possible. What complicated this simplification was that I could not stand to hurt other people, even when they deserved it. Also, I found that it was easier to lie to them than to argue. In fact, I agreed with most people just to shut them up. And because I agreed with whatever they said, people who didn't really know me believed that I thought just as they did. People who knew me better thought I was a flake because, inevitably, I contradicted myself.

I learned to survive by going with the flow, and I always took the path of least resistance. For example, I calculated that the certainty of losing a toe would be better than the uncertainty of going into combat, and then I pulled the trigger.

Of course, I did consider other options. If it had not been my toe that got me out of the army, it probably would have been a Section Eight. To this end, I had confessed to the Army shrink my fear of Oscar, my parents' German Shepherd. The dog had persecuted me throughout my childhood.

The shrink, of course, understood my fear clearly.

"You see, Eddie," he said, "you have a phobia rooted deep in your libido. It's really not Oscar you're afraid of, but your latent homosexuality."

"But I'm not a homo—"

"You have to stop denying it! You have to confront your demons!"

"I didn't say anything about demons."

"Now, Eddie. We've discussed these paranoid delusions of yours concerning your parents' dog. It's really not the dog at all. You're crying out for love and acceptance. Confront your demons, Eddie, and Oscar won't bother you anymore."

I considered where the doctor was going with this line of reasoning, and I decided to shoot off my toe.

On the day I returned home to Southern California, Oscar recognized me immediately and attacked. As I stepped up to the front door, Oscar had the seat of my britches between his teeth and was getting dangerously close to my *huevos rancheros*.

My mother answered the door and Oscar let go.

"Yes?" she asked, fumbling with her glasses.

By the time she got her glasses in place, the asshole dog was wagging his tail and licking my hand.

"Eddie!" She seemed pleased, and then she turned to the dog. "Yes, yes, Oscar. Eddie's home. You're happy to see him, aren't you, boy?"

She took me by the arm and led me, a little too quickly, into the house. I limped slightly as we entered the living room, where my father sat in front of the TV. They noticed the limp and a look of concern crossed their faces.

Never one to show his emotions, my father muffled his greetings and said nothing about my limp. I noticed that he had gained a

7

considerable amount of weight since I'd seen him last.

"Is it bad?" asked my mother with a worried quiver in her voice.

"No. Sometimes I don't notice it at all. They say I'll compensate and find my balance."

My father gathered himself quickly.

"I'm sure you don't want to talk about it, Son," he said. "So, have you any plans? For the future?"

"Oh, Lazlo! Let the boy get comfortable before you lay into him," said my mother. She turned to go into the kitchen.

"Geezus H. Christ, Millie! I got a right to know," replied my father, craning his neck in my mother's direction. "Who pays the bills around here, anyways?"

He looked back at me, expectantly.

"I figured I would kind of take it easy for a while, Dad. I'm not yet used to this war wound."

"Well, don't dwell on it. You fall off a horse, you gotta get right back on him."

"Where are we going to keep a horse, Lazlo?" ridiculed my mother, returning from the kitchen with a pitcher of lemonade.

My father ignored her and continued.

"There's a lot of boys far worse off who've made good."

My mother removed her glasses. She seemed to be considering my father's statement.

"Look at Helen Keller," she declared. "She was blind and deaf, yet she learned to be useful. She had a positive attitude."

But a positive attitude was elusive for the time being. I soon discovered that, in my absence, my parents had taken the liberty of giving away all my prized possessions—albums, posters and the typical assortment of paraphernalia valued by a generation I no longer felt connected to.

To make matters worse, my father had let my car fall into disarray. The tires on my VW bug were completely flat, and the battery was dead, so when I wanted to go into town, I had to take my old bicycle.

At first I thought it a blessing in disguise. With the wind in my face, I glided happily along, reliving the simple pleasures of my youth. Abruptly my euphoria came to a halt when I heard the burst of a siren.

To make a long story short, I was cited by a cop for having a broken bicycle reflector. Later, as I held the ticket in my hand, my disappointment grew. Defiantly, I threw it away—an act I later came to regret.

But at the time my biggest disappointment was that all of my friends were gone. Being away from home for the first time, I had fantasized what it would be like seeing my old buddies—all the bragging and lying. But they had gone their separate ways. All of them except Conrad Christopher.

Conrad. Here was another disappointment altogether. But Winston would have loved him. It was Conrad's idea that I go to college.

I was reluctant to see him at first. There was more than a little bad blood between us. He had stolen my manic-depressive girlfriend, Carry Ann Fowl, and married her. I didn't think he would ever forgive me for that.

But after several days of doing nothing and going nowhere, I decided that having a half-assed friend was better than having none at all.

"They say all over town you're some kind of war hero, Eddie," he said, as we walked down the quiet tree-lined street near his apartment.

"Well," I mumbled modestly, "it's no big deal. I did what I had to do. Knowing you, you would have probably done the same thing."

Behind the cover of an overgrown pepper tree, Conrad produced a large, yellow bomber. He lit it with a ceremonious motion, his hand cupped over the burning end of the joint, and sucked in the smoke deeply.

"Have you thought about what you're gonna do now that you're home?" he asked, handing it to me.

"You too? My father's been giving me the daily third degree about my future."

"Well, Carry and I kind of wondered what you would do when you came home," he said, exhaling the potent vapors. "Carry says you're a bum. But then, no one would ever have dreamed that you would come home a hero. Maybe you'll surprise her."

I inhaled and thought about Carry. According to her, I was a total screw-up. Maybe I was, but Carry, regardless of what Conrad wanted to believe, only hated me because I refused to marry her, despite how much money her father had.

I passed the joint back to Conrad and sized him up.

9

Even if Carry had never entered the picture, Conrad and I would still have had a strained friendship. He could never believe that I really didn't want to be like him. He had a personality sculpted by greed and ambition—a candidate for executive ulcers, high blood pressure, and a headstone fit for the richest dead man in the cemetery. He was the only person I ever knew who carried a photograph of his car in his wallet.

My goals in life were very different from Conrad's. I liked money just as much as he did, but he would do anything for it. He even married for it. Of course, by now he must have realized that he was going to earn every penny of it. Carry was no free ride.

What made me different from Conrad was not so much what I wanted; it was what I *didn't* want. I did not want responsibility for anything. My goals had always been quite simple: to sleep late, eat what I wanted, go where I wanted, and do as I pleased. That was why I hated the army so much. And that was why I didn't want to confound my life by getting married.

"Have you thought about going to college?" Conrad asked.

This was the kind of suggestion Conrad knew would irritate me. I had been a horrible student, and he knew it. I suspected that he was trying to rub the past in my face.

"Think about it, Eddie. College fits your life style. Don't forget, you're now entitled to the GI Bill, right?"

"Cut the crap, Conrad. You know I was a pretty lousy student. What college would accept me?"

"Hell," he said. "I'm not talking about Harvard. There are plenty of state colleges that would probably take you. Besides, you can always plead minority. You've got the right surname. They'll let you in. They're looking for Mexicans. Haven't you heard of affirmative action?"

The irony staggered me. In high school they had put me in retard classes. They assumed that because my last name was Delano, I couldn't speak English. But I wasn't angry about what they did. Underestimating me had suited me fine because I was rarely assigned any homework.

"My grades were really bad, Conrad. I don't think affirmative action would make that big of a difference."

"Then tell 'em you're black. There you go. With a Mexican surname and you telling them you're black, they gotta let you in."

10

This kind of angling was exactly the kind of thing Winston would have loved about Conrad. But I knew the way Conrad's mind reasoned, and I didn't like it. To him there were degrees of racial depravity. To be of Mexican heritage meant you were only partially screwed up. To be black meant you were a little more screwed up. Being both meant you had to be so screwed up that society owed you something and had to let you into college.

I thought about confronting him on this issue. But that would have required a lot of effort, and it hardly seemed worthwhile. Besides, people couldn't really be changed unless they wanted to be. The best way of dealing with someone like Conrad was to be practical.

I thanked him for his suggestion and told him I would think about it. In fact, I did think about it, and once past the insulting innuendo, I discovered it really wasn't a bad idea. What did I have to lose if I told the college I was both black and Hispanic?

Indeed, while lying on my back in the hospital contemplating the loss of my big toe, I had come to the realization that life was a game in which, in the end, no one won much of anything. But that was acceptable. And if there were any rules, they were vague. A person could be a victim of circumstance, or he could make up his own rules.

And maybe, if he was lucky, he could have a little fun along the way.

2

Bulla-Bulla

It was hard to believe that Conrad's idea would work. Even he was surprised when I told him I was leaving for college. How any school would accept me, even if it was under the strict conditions of academic probation, was a miracle.

I have credited part of my success to the scientific means I employed in choosing an institution of higher learning. First, the college had to be far away. That way my parents and friends wouldn't bother me. Second, for obvious reasons, it had to be cheap. I then closed my eyes and planted my finger somewhere on the map of Northern California. The nearest qualifying college to where my finger had landed was Del Norte State.

A catalogue of courses and registration forms for the spring semester were sent to me. Among the materials was a brochure with a photograph on the cover of a number of large brick buildings surrounded by vineyards, rolling hills and patches of forest.

The photograph drew my mother's attention.

"It looks lovely," she said, examining the glossy photoprint. "I'm going to put this on the refrigerator door."

And there it remained until the day I left for college.

Several days after receiving my letter of acceptance from Del Norte, I received another formal letter from the college. My mother brought it to me in the garage where I was attaching a bicycle rack to my VW.

I was about to put the letter aside unopened when my mother's curiosity got the best of her. She seized it from my hands, opened it and began to mumble the words to herself until she reached a certain part of the letter that she decided needed to be read aloud:

The Black Student Union will be at your
service whenever you need us. We are here
to help you. If you need tutoring, financial
assistance or simply new friends who share
your needs and concerns, we are here for
you.

She looked impressed.

"Well, you can't say those colored people aren't gracious."

"Mom, I think they prefer to be called black."

"What difference does it make. You didn't receive anything like this from any white student union. You should be grateful."

On the day I arrived at Del Norte, it was overcast. Thunder rolled above the dark, heavy clouds that filled the sky from one end of the valley to the other. Soon it began to shower, and visibility in the valley diminished.

I found the campus housing office in a long trailer in the middle of a muddy field. After squeezing my way through a crowd of students, most of them returning from their semester break, I found myself behind a cute girl who was copying information from the few posted cards on a large corkboard.

One of the bearded student employees, who looked to me exactly like most of the other male students, worked his way through the crowd and made an announcement.

"If you please stand back for a moment, I will read out loud the remainder of the available housing."

Space was made for him. He settled himself next to the wall where the rentals were posted and pulled the remaining cards off of the board one at a time. He read the first card.

"Eco-feminist, looking for female nonsmoker."

Several hands shot up. He passed the card to the nearest one, an attractive blonde.

"Bisexual, vegetarian, prefers AC/DC female roommate—must be neat."

There was a minor disturbance in the crowd as a short, stocky girl plowed her way forward and grabbed the card.

13

"Neo-Trotskyite, into espresso and late night raps. Looking for comrade of equal persuasion. No FBI agents please."

A clenched fist shot up, and a guy in a beret and camouflage field jacket took the card.

"Reformed heroin addict—honest, I am—looking for responsible roommate with a job."

A straight-looking guy next to me spoke up, "I got a job!" He moved forward to take the card.

"Born-again Mary, looking for young Christians in need of spiritual haven. Regular church attendance mandatory. No sex, no drugs, no rock and roll."

"Fuck that," said the cute girl in front of me. There were no takers and the student worker tacked the card back up on the board. He continued.

"Neo-Buddhist, semi-vegitarian, into drugs—"

"That's it!" said the cute girl. She rushed forward to claim the index card.

"Converted chicken coop, no power no water."

I grew impatient as the student employee droned on.

"Trailer in back of supermarket, no toilet," he paused. "And that's about it."

The crowd moaned. The speaker quickly angled his way back to his desk, stood upon a chair, and spoke above the din.

"Come back tomorrow after one o'clock," he said grimly. "Sometimes we get more."

The crowd rushed by me, forcing me aside, and I found myself next to the worker's desk.

When the student worker stepped down off the chair, an attractive brunette with a red scarf came forward.

"Winston sent me," she whispered.

The student worker smiled and offered her a black ledger. The brunette leisurely scanned it, wrote something down, thanked him, and then headed for the door.

What I had just witnessed baffled me. Was this preferential treatment, inside dealing, or perhaps something else? Who was this Winston?

Of course, the brunette *was* cute. So who could blame the student worker for favoring her? And I figured if I questioned him, he might be offended, thereby making it even harder to find decent

14

housing. It seemed best to leave quietly, keeping my observation to myself.

The rain had stopped, so I walked around the campus. I was impressed by the stately brick buildings, tree-lined pathways, and manicured lawns. But most impressive were the many young coeds. I felt I could get to like Del Norte, if I could only find a place to live.

Still in search of housing, I found myself in a dingy part of town, on a corner that can best be described as the Baltic Avenue and Mediterranean Place of this great Monopoly board of life. There I found a small coffee house called Fernie's Hideaway that catered to students. I was told that sometimes they posted housing rentals.

There were no posted rentals, but there were young women with long, unkempt hair—some wearing overalls, others in shapeless granny dresses—sitting at the tables and sipping espresso. Various flyers cluttered the tables and counters. I examined one of them.

"Down with third-world exploitation—New People's Army."

Then I noticed an angry-looking young man watching me from across the room. I assumed he was gay. He was wearing an earring.

His shrewd expression made me feel uncomfortable. I was about to toss the flier when I realized he was studying me. I decided to put it in my pocket instead, and he approved of this by nodding and smiling knowingly.

I still felt uncomfortable and left before a waitress took my order. This turned out to be a timely stroke of luck. Across the street from Fernie's, an old white-haired man was attaching a *For Rent* sign to a courtyard fence surrounding a cluster of wood-framed bungalows. The place looked to be a dump. But my experience at the student housing office told me that I could not afford to be picky.

As I approached, the old man studied me. He winced when he noticed my limp, and I could see the sympathy in his kind eyes. A fringe benefit from shooting off my toe.

"How much?" I asked, nodding towards the sign.

"A hundred-and-ten dollars a month," said the old man.

"That's about half my GI check," I thought aloud.

"Oh," he said with a note of enthusiasm in his voice. "You're on the GI Bill. Make it ninety. Can you handle that?"

"Yeah," I said. "I can economize and get by."

"You'll do nothing of the sort. You're a veteran! Did you hurt your leg in the war?"

15

"Uh, yeah. Nam," I said modestly.

"Eighty-five bucks a month. No last month or cleaning deposit."

I followed him to his porch, signed the rental agreement and paid him on the spot. He then stood at attention and saluted me.

"Veteran—WWII!"

I returned the salute out of politeness.

Though the power was yet to be turned on and it was cold and dark in my new place, it was a lot better than sleeping in my car. I lay awake fantasizing about the possibilities of college life. However, there was something peculiar about Del Norte. I could not put my finger on it, but it wasn't enough to spoil my optimism. I slept soundly that first night.

The following morning as I stood at the entrance of the student store, it hit me. Embedded in bronze on the wall before me was the school logo. It was of a bloodshot eye bordered by the words, *En Tedium Boredumus E Mediocriti.*

I had seen it before, on my registration forms and brochures, but I had never paid close attention to it. Now, as I walked around inside the store, I realized that the logo was on everything, from tee shirts and book covers to sweat shirts and gym shorts.

That wasn't the only thing that struck me as peculiar. On every wall were posters of organizations, like the "Hands Off Guacamole Committee." This poster portrayed Uncle Sam eating a piece of Central America. But the oddest poster was that of a smiling fat man with a beard, under whom were the words, "Peace and Contentment Through Baba Rama."

I returned my attention to my original purpose, which was to buy an updated catalogue of courses. I noticed that more than a few of the textbook shelves were depleted. Several had signs that read, "Need books? See Winston."

"Who the hell is this Winston?" I thought aloud.

I took my place in line at the cash register to purchase the catalogue of courses.

"You new here?" asked a friendly student. He had the customary long hair and beard.

"Why, yes. How'd you know?"

He didn't have to say it. I was probably the only shorthaired, clean-shaved male student on campus.

"You have that bewildered look on your face." He smiled, then added, "You'll like it here. It's real laid back. No bull, like at other schools. There *was* a student government. They met a year ago and did two things—they banned football, and then they banned student government. We're now the hotbed of apathy. With the exception of the New People's Army."

"I've seen their posters. Who are they?"

"Who knows? They just, like, strike out of nowhere. Sometimes they break windows. Once they set fire to a toolshed. On another occasion they let the air out of a custodian's tires."

"Have they hurt anyone?"

"No. They protest third-world exploitation and advocate peace and controlled terrorism. I really don't follow them much. I'm kind of committed to a noncommittal sort of view of the world."

I tagged along with him to the Student Union Building where we met a group of his friends. One of the guys seemed overjoyed to see my new companion.

"Winston got me into that closed class," he said excitedly.

"Cool," said my new friend, as we joined them at the large table.

"Who's this Winston?" I asked. "Everywhere I go I hear his name."

"He's cool," said one of the other guys, with a slight note of condescension.

"He's an asshole," said another.

"He's really cute," said one of the girls, to the chagrin of her boyfriend, the guy who had got into the closed class.

None of their comments on this Winston answered my question, and my new friend, who now seemed to be ignoring me, redirected the conversation to a different topic. So I returned to skimming my spring catalogue for possible classes. At a lull in the conversation, I spoke up.

"Any of you know this guy Pearson? Teaches psych."

"You don't wanna take that class," said one of the long-haired guys with an especially scraggly beard. He added, in a slow nasal intonation, "That guy gives homework."

"Yeah, he's real traditional," said a girl sitting next to him. "I mean, it's mellow if that's what you're into."

"I'd check into some of the other classes," another girl suggested. "Like, there's this class we're taking on comparative sun signs. It's an acceptable substitute for Astronomy 1A."

"I've signed up for an alternative class called You and Your Mantra," said the first girl.

"Neither sounds very academic," I said, realizing too late my thoughtlessness.

"Don't get judgmental," the first girl said coolly. "If you can't relate to it, that's *your* uptight, middle-class problem!"

I felt as if I had just farted in front of all of them. Unwelcome stares and a silence followed. They were all too nonjudgmental to ask me to leave, but I knew I wasn't wanted.

Within a few minutes I was standing in the registration line, which moved with unexpected speed. I soon found myself before a middle-aged woman wearing horn-rimmed glasses.

"Your file isn't on record," she said in a lifeless voice.

"But I have this letter saying I was accepted."

She examined it.

"Perhaps there's been a mistake. It is possible that your papers are misplaced. Let me explain, Mr. Delano," she said as she peered above her glasses. "Del Norte has a unique filing system. Instead of dehumanizing you students by assigning numbers, we categorize you according to your astrological charts."

She looked at my date of birth.

"Oh, I see what the problem is. You've been listed as an Aries with a moon in Libra, but you're actually a Pisces in Leo. No wonder you seem so confused."

She stepped to a file cabinet, pulled out a folder and examined the contents. She looked puzzled, peered at me over her glasses, and returned holding the folder.

"I'm at a loss for words. Your registration forms are at the Black Student Union."

The Black Student Union was not easy to find, but find it I did. It was across the street from the main campus in an old storefront, between the *All Children Rich and Smart Preschool* and the *Tenth Evangelical Church of Jesus Christ*. Its walls were covered with posters of Eldridge Cleaver and Huey Newton. The Newton poster portrayed him as an armed revolutionary, wearing bandoleers and cradling a shotgun in his arms.

Enthroned behind the registration table at the back of the room sat an angry black youth with a fiery Afro sticking out from beneath a black beret.

"What can I help you with?" he said mockingly.

"I was told my registration forms were here."

"There must be some kind of mistake, friend. This registration table is for the brothers and sisters."

I was about to insist that he at least make an effort to see if my forms were on file, but something made me ask, "Why are you doing your registration over here?"

"You see, we are tired of being the objects of racial discrimination. In order to avoid racial segregation, we have separated ourselves from the rest of the student population. Can you dig it?"

"Yeah, man," I lied. "But you're still segregated."

"That's the typical bourgeois response one expects to hear from a member of the ruling-class, mad-dog, racist, lackey muthafuckers!"

"How true. Nevertheless, can you check out your files? It's either under Edward Delano or Pisces in Leo."

"Did Winston send you?" he asked with a smirk.

There it was again—Winston.

"What if he did?"

"No problem." He retrieved a stack of folders. "Can you believe this shit? That damned Winston! Here it is. And here you go, brother."

"Right on, brother."

My first class filled to its limit. A good sign, I thought. Must be a popular professor.

The teacher, Dr. Bergman, was a balding middle-aged man with a big red nose that had large pores reminiscent of those on an orange. His puffy red cheeks revealed the tiny red corpuscle lines of alcoholism.

Within moments of distributing the course syllabus, Dr. Bergman fell asleep at his desk. The students examined one another, as if they had anticipated the event. When Bergman snored loudly enough, most of the students slipped out of class. I sat quietly for a moment, then someone whispered.

19

"Hey you."

I turned around and saw a student wearing sunglasses and smiling at me. He summoned me to follow him. As we walked down the hall, he laughed.

"Bergman's got narcolepsy. This class is gonna be a breeze."

I had to admit I was impressed. This was going to be much better than I expected. Yes, both the students *and* the professors were lazy and weird. But all this meant was that I was not going to be expected to do much. I could see that I was going to waltz my way through college. On top of that, the GI Bill was paying me for being here.

And this was just the beginning. Just as I thought things could not get any better, my next class proved otherwise.

I sat directly in front of the lectern as the class began to fill with students. Finally, a disheveled looking man with at least a three-day growth bristling on his face entered. He wore a threadbare, gray V-necked sweater and a stained white shirt with a red and green tie loosened at the collar. He placed a weathered briefcase on the desk directly behind the lectern. As he stood with his back to us taking some papers from a folder, I could see his shirttail hanging out from below his sweater.

He turned around, avoiding eye contact with students, and said, "I'mmm. I'm your spee-spee-speech teacher, Profe-fe-fesor Wilson." His eyes jetted to the ceiling, as if the mere sight of his students would be a fate worse than death. "I'mmm sor-sor-sorry about the ca-ca-cost of your te-te-texts."

He paused for a moment before looking quickly down at his shoes. He whispered, "Pua-pua-public speaking is," he grasped the edge of the lectern and spoke louder, "can be," and then he shouted, "a terrifying ex-ex-experience!"

He then seemed to become aware of the fact that he was addressing his shoes. He jerked his head up and stared at the class. His eyes bulged in utter terror.

"You can bring in a sur-sur-surrogate speaker if you-you-you wish."

Then he shifted into an indignant voice.

"Making people speak against their will is bulla-bulla-bullshit!"

3

The Woman's Movement

The biggest drawback with going to college was not having more money. But even that was not the real problem. The real problem was that with an absence of money came the absence of a social life, and with the absence of a social life came the absence of a sex life.

Now, conventional wisdom would suggest that if money was an obstacle to having a social life, ergo a sex life, one should find a job. The problem with working, beyond the obvious fact that all jobs really sucked, was that jobs required time. So a person might very well have a job and make good money, but then he had another problem: he had no time to spend his money. And when he finally got time, he was generally too tired to do anything.

But more to the point, my classes were a lot more work than I had figured. So I didn't have the time to be social. And when I did have the time between semesters, I didn't have the money.

Early in my third semester, I became obsessed with the fear that if I didn't break away and find a girl, I'd go bald and my voice would rise to a high falsetto.

And the longer this obsession went untreated, the more driven I became. I'd stare longingly from the library window at the shapely forms of females walking by with that irresistible female wiggle. With so many of them out there, it had to be easy, but it wasn't. Being saddled with this obsession‚ had made me painfully self-conscious.

What made this problem worse was that a lot of women seemed to be angry at men. And I saw what this anger could do firsthand. I saw what it did to the men in my Hemingway class.

Dr. Wilter seemed out of place teaching Hemingway. He carried himself like the quiet scholarly type. Shelly would have been more fitting. I shouldn't say it, but he even looked a little like a wuss. And he was the last person on campus I would have suspected of being sexist.

On the first day of class, just after he distributed the syllabus, a group of young women, most of them with hairy legs and thick eyebrows, walked out in a quiet huff. It seemed that no one else had noticed their departure. I did so only because one of the girls wore tight Levi's and had a cute ass. I was disappointed to see her leave so suddenly.

The reason for their departure became apparent at our next class meeting. Wilter, apparently perplexed, fumbled for words.

"I apologize. According to Dr. Hartstone, a number of you have complained that I've failed to include any women authors in our reading list. I'd like to say in my defense, this course *was* supposed to be an introduction to Hemingway. But, on your insistence, we've made it a seminar. And now, in the interest of fairness, I've added a female author to the course outline."

The Frida Kahlo look-alikes cheered; Wilter looked ill.

"From this point on, the course will be a Hemingway *and* Willa Cather seminar," he said, distributing an updated syllabus.

The following week Dr. Hartstone, a big blonde woman who wore men's suits, ushered the angry women into class. Cornering Wilter, she spoke.

"It's come to my attention that you have a number of highly gifted young women in your class who would like to see more of a balance in your reading list."

"I've already added a female author."

"Yes, but women have been an oppressed gender for so long that we believe a counterbalance is necessary, and you should add at least one more woman author to your reading list," said Hartstone.

The babe with the cute ass spoke up.

"Why can't we make this a Willa Cather/Virginia Woolf/Hemingway seminar?"

The wheels of Wilter's mind must have been grinding to a halt. His face turned red. The veins in his forehead were bursting.

"Of course, in the spirit of fairness," he offered with a strained smile.

It seemed to me that he was bending over backwards. But it was not enough to appease the group of lesbian separatists, who threatened a school-wide boycott if more courses on female authors were not offered immediately.

By the fourth week, Hemingway was out altogether; so were Wilter and all the male students. Uninformed about the change in the program, I walked into class and found out how angry a lot of women could be. The new professor, a beast of a woman, screamed at me.

"This class is closed to all men! Leave now or I'll have campus security remove you!"

It was for the best. I could see I wasn't going to get laid in that class anyway.

There were changes taking place between men and women that confused me. If you liked women, you had to like them for their minds. But I couldn't help but notice their bodies. This weakness, I was beginning to feel, made me some kind of pervert.

My luck with women was getting progressively worse. For example, there was a girl named Peggy who sat next to me in my art history class. She seemed friendly enough. She smiled when our eyes made contact. When my nerve at last came, I asked her what she was doing Saturday night.

"Nothing, with you," she said, and from that day forth she sat as far away from me as she could.

Later, a second girl replied to the same question, "I'm sorry, but my dog needs a shampoo."

But the best excuse for not going out with me came from a girl in my astronomy class.

"Gee, I'd like to, but I'm leaving for Paraguay next year."

The rejection, coupled with the obsession for sex, had me looking for hair on the palms of my hands.

What made all this even worse was that, in spite of all these angry women, some of the guys on campus seemed to be doing all right. I didn't get it. I felt I was doing something wrong.

Then I discovered a fundamental truth: The law of averages redeems the persistent.

This principle didn't just happen. I first had to be honest with myself. I had to admit that I was, at best, a one percenter. That meant that I could only score on about one percent of the female population I asked out.

But that didn't mean I was a loser. I'd just have to work a little harder. I figured that if I hit on a hundred girls a week, I should score with at least one of them, and that wasn't so bad.

It seemed ironic, but after assuming a philosophical outlook on women, my luck changed in—of all classes—philosophy. It must have been metaphysical.

She was a sweet young brunette. Whenever I tried to make eye contact with her, I blushed with the embarrassment of my own wicked thoughts. Then one day she returned eye contact and smiled coyly. My imagination ran wild. From that moment on she became more than just a highly-rated face in the crowded pageant of females I had fallen in lust with.

But something wasn't quite right about her, and I couldn't put my finger on it. Perhaps it was that she too often argued with the professor, which wasn't half as troubling as the fact that she always managed to bring the arguments around to the same single issue: the women's movement.

Professor Holden on this day was discussing Plato and was about to move on to another chapter in our text, *Trivial Issues in Philosophy*, when she stood up angrily and waved her hand.

"Excuse me, excuse me! Sir, Professor!" she said. Then she grabbed the back of the chair in front of her and leaned forward in a way that accentuated her lovely ass.

A look of resignation crossed Holden's face, as if he were a bank robber whose nearly clean getaway was foiled by a cop who had been waiting in ambush. He could not ignore her.

Reluctantly, Professor Holden replied, "Yes, Debbie?"

Angling her body, apparently to find a more comfortable stance, she tilted her hips to the left, shifting her perfectly formed butt. She did all of this in one graceful motion as she asked her question.

"Just how *did* Plato see women in his Republic?"

I didn't know what Holden was going to say about Plato's view of women, but if Plato had the view I now had of Debbie's rear, he would have held them in fairly high esteem.

"I would like to know how Plato saw women in his Republic!" she repeated adamantly.

"Young lady, you have managed to turn every issue in this class into a feminist forum. I'm no longer going to allow you to move us from our topic."

"I demand an answer!"

"Who gives a shit!" said my stately professor.

Gasping and murmuring erupted among the students. Debbie fled the room, a fractious air about her. A group of like-minded women followed her out of class; then one of them, who I recognized from my former Hemingway/Cather/Woolf seminar, hesitated at the door and yelled.

"You sexist pig! This is not the last you'll hear of this, you chauvinist!"

Holden canceled class for the day.

It was warm enough to sit on the grass just outside the student union, so I picked out a spot that would allow me to watch the girls go by. As I sat, I heard someone crying just a few feet away. It was Debbie, and she was alone. I saw an opportunity and I moved closer to her.

"Hey, is everything all right?" I asked with feigned sincerity.

"No! Um, yes. I'm okay. Thank you for asking."

We made eye contact. Recognition crossed her face, and she smiled.

"You're the guy who sits two rows behind me."

Something rang hollow in her enthusiasm, but I didn't care. I was feeling lucky, so I sat down next to her.

"Are you sure you're okay?"

She sighed with resignation.

"You saw what I just did. I made a fool of myself!"

"No you didn't," I lied. "I'm sure it'll blow over by tomorrow."

"Holden is such a sexist pig! He had no right to say that."

"No, it wasn't appropriate."

What was not appropriate was her behavior, but I would not share that with her. Besides, she was smiling again, and my heart was pounding rapidly.

I had to think fast. A better opportunity would not arise, so I kept on lying, "You know, I think you were right."

She responded with an warm expression that encouraged me to continue.

"That rat Plato was probably a real sexist. I bet that's the reason Holden didn't want to get into it."

"That's what I was thinking, too." She relaxed. Her eyes were re-assessing me. "You know, I think I like you. You seem so different."

The moment she said it, I had an instant erection.

25

"You don't seem like the kind of man who's threatened by the women's movement."

I shrugged my shoulders and she continued.

"You don't seem like the kind of guy who has nothing but sex on his mind."

"Well," I said modestly, "once in a while, I guess."

"You wouldn't be normal if you didn't once in a while." She smiled coyly and then added cautiously, "You're cute."

My heart palpitated and my face felt warm. This was all moving too fast. I was not in control of the situation. But that was okay.

She smiled, "I've got some wine at my place. It's not far from here. We can get to know each other."

We finished several glasses of wine, and I moved closer for a gentle, persuasive kiss, followed by the soft touch of my hands fondling her body, exploring all regions with excitement.

Then the peeling away of clothing, soft brushes of bare skin, and impulsive groping. Hot kisses devouring soft shoulders, orally praising supple breasts, commending the sleek smooth curves of her body. She moaned her approval.

And then the woman's movement.

Soon afterward, she left for the bathroom. I relished the moments between her sheets. I could get used to this. Debbie had a certain bold quality I liked. Maybe this thing with her could go a little further.

Then a pang from my empty stomach distracted me from my thoughts and, impulsively, I called out to her.

"Hey, Debbie. Would you like to get something to eat?"

She returned to the bedroom wearing a floral dress.

"How'd you know my name?"

The question seemed odd. I sensed a defensiveness in her voice.

"That's what Holden called you," I said with a smile. Then I added, "We're in the same class, remember?"

"Right. But I didn't give you my name. I never give it to any of the guys I fuck, unless I want to make something of it."

"I thought you liked me."

"I don't want you to get any ideas."

"Ideas? I just thought that maybe we could be friends."

"And then what? I know your type. You think just because someone's been intimate with you, you own them!"

"No, I just—"

"I think it's time for you to leave."

"But I thought that when a man and a woman made love, there might be something special between them."

"That's a sexist way of looking at relationships. It's okay for men to score on women, but when women do it to men, it's wrong."

"What?"

"Get out of my apartment! Now, you sexist!"

I wasn't entirely sure of what I did or said that made her so angry, but I knew there was no point in asking her for another date.

At least the hair on the palms of my hands were gone.

4

Sam

The next morning I was rudely awaken from the soundest sleep I'd had in months by the shrill sound of a woman's voice. At first I thought it was Debbie, but it turned out to be my landlord's wife. They were arguing about money.

"Huxley, I need—no, let me restate that—I *deserve* new furniture!"

"What's wrong with what we have now?"

"Gloria Shulman's husband bought her new furniture. Early American! Exactly what I've begged you for the last fifteen years!"

"So now we're keeping up with the Shulmans. Where do you expect me to get the money to keep up with the Shulmans?"

"Where do you think?" she said with hostile sarcasm. "The tenants!"

"They're struggling students. They don't have two nickels to rub together."

"Huxley, I have my heart set on Early American!"

Needless to say, Huxley lost the argument, and I was left with three choices: I could cut out the utilities, cut out eating, or find a roommate. I decided I could not give up my utilities, and giving up food wouldn't last long, so I decided to give up my privacy.

I returned to the infamous student housing office. I read the cards on the wall:

"Virgo with moon in Leo looking for Cancer with Scorpio rising. Male student with new stereo system looking for a female roommate—no dogs. Gay Christian looking for young man—must be ecologically concerned. Born-again Mary—no sex, no drugs, no rock'n'roll—Irish need not apply."

There was no competition.

I scribbled on a handful of three-by-five index cards, "Reasonable human looking for another reasonable human for roommate." The first one to respond appeared at my door the next day. He was a stoned, bearded young man. Before me stood someone who had lost many brain cells—a casualty of the psychedelic generation. He spoke with that lazy nasal intonation that could only mean he was stoned out of his mind.

"Say, man, are you the reasonable human? Who needs a reasonable human roommate?"

"That's me," I said.

"Far-fucking-out, dude. I'm a real reasonable guy, too. I really dig the way you put it, man."

"Well, can you tell me about yourself?"

"Sure, man. Wha'da ya wanna know?"

"What's your name?"

"Sam." He smiled.

"Are you a student at Del Norte?"

"I dropped outta college, 'cause it's just not relative to life, man. You know what I mean? It's just not relative. Can you dig it?"

Out of politeness I lied, "Why don't you come back in a few days after I've made a decision?"

"Right, man. I can dig it. You gotta make a decision."

Within an hour a second person knocked on my door. She was an overweight young woman in a large, shapeless granny dress. She looked surprised when she saw me.

"Oh, you're a man! I didn't know you were a man!"

"I'm sorry, I—"

"You're a man! Your card at the student housing center said *reasonable* human being. But you're a *man*! I'm going to report you for false advertising!"

The following day, just as I was about to leave for school, another applicant appeared at my door. He was a politico, and he immediately told me what he was looking for.

"Something that's progressive and communal. We can share our food and other responsibilities."

"Share our food? I only need a roommate."

"Yeah, sharing. And as soon as I get some money, I can help out on my end."

"You don't have an income?"

29

"Not exactly. You see, I'm into this free-flowing, communal life style. Working is definitely a reactionary mind-set."

"I couldn't agree more, but just how do you intend to pay the rent?"

"I was counting on you, comrade. I'm putting all of my energy into getting the US imperialists out of the People's Democratic Republic of Guacamole."

"What the hell..."

"You never heard of it? I'm with the Hands Off Guacamole Committee. It's my whole life's work."

"I thought guacamole was something you eat."

"That's a racial slur if I ever heard one!"

After a parade of six or seven mental oddballs came to see me about the possibility of being my "reasonable" roommate, I realized there were problems I had not expected.

One vegetarian said, "You eat meat? Oh no. Not in this day and age! Don't you realize that you are eating animals?"

"Yes, dead ones."

Horror crossed his face.

"Animals are our friends," he said with a plea for mercy in his voice.

The next one almost hit me for owning a car.

"You're screwing up the environment with that evil thing!"

"It's just a car. I mean—"

"Guys like you are blind to the realities of our environment."

He walked away at an angry pace. I saw him reach the corner, where he hitched a quick ride and was gone.

When the first applicant, Sam, returned, I was happy to see him.

"Do you still got the room to rent, man?"

"Yes, Sam. But I'd like to ask you a few questions before I make a final decision."

"Sure, man, I can dig it," he said. "You gotta know who you're getting involved with, right dude? I mean, for all you know I could be an ax murderer, or a Satan worshipper, or a Nazi."

"Something like that, Sam."

"Hell, I could be some kind of pervert or something, who's got all kinds of weird—"

"Enough!" I shouted.

He hung his head low.

"I've annoyed you, haven't I? Sometimes I overdo things. Tell me the truth. I can take it."

"Please, don't feel bad." I could not hurt his feelings, so I quickly added, "Just answer these questions. Do you share solidarity with the People's Republic of Guacamole?"

"What the hell is that, dude?"

"No problem. Do you think cars are destroying the environment?"

"Hell, I don't know. These are trick questions aren't they?" A hurt, pensive expression crossed his face as he said, "I've blown it, haven't I? Tell me the truth."

"No, you're doing fine, really. I'm impressed. One last question."

With a renewed sense of confidence, he smiled and said, "Fire away, man."

"Do you have a job, or a means of income?"

"Yeah, man, I got a job."

"It seems to me that you've got all the right qualities for being a roommate."

"Thanks, man! You won't regret this decision. It'll be the best thing you ever did. Really, man. One day I'm gonna return the favor. Really."

"Enough, Sam!"

"No, really, man. You won't regret this."

I was already beginning to have second thoughts. Sam must have seen it in my face.

"Okay. Thanks," he said with two short bursts, and then he closed his mouth and sealed his lips like a zipper with his finger. "Not another word."

Sam had a job at a kennel. He didn't earn much, but money wasn't his major concern. Just as long as he had enough to pay the rent and buy marijuana, Sam was a happy man.

Occasionally, he'd ask, "You wanna smoke some dope?"

"Nah. I'm trying to quit."

Whenever I had the urge to smoke some weed, I'd just look at Sam, and the urge would disappear.

After several months of sharing the bungalow with him, I began to realize that I had underestimated him. Indeed, he was a highly-evolved thinker who had come to terms with himself.

He once told me, while we sat on the porch drinking beer, "You know, I really dig my career. I know a lot of guys just couldn't dig it. I mean, dog shit, right? That's the first thing that comes to everyone's mind when you tell them you work in a kennel. But it isn't all dog shit. Some of those dogs really get to you."

He took a long, deep swig from his bottle and then continued.

"Sometimes I go to work, smoke a doobie, and I can almost swear those dogs are talking to me. You know, they really depend on me, Eddie."

"Interesting, Sam. I'm glad you've found a calling in life."

"Say, there's an opening for a part-time worker. You interested? I can pull some strings and get you in. The boss and me are real tight."

"No, I don't like dogs."

"You don't? How come?"

"It's a long story. Besides, I can't see myself working like that."

"Sure you can. You just need a positive outlook."

"I just don't have the zeal for it the way you do. I mean, you like dogs, and it wouldn't bother you to do it for the rest of your life, but—"

"Hey, don't get me wrong. I can't see doing this for the rest of my life. But, you know, it's not every man who can find satisfaction in his job."

Unfortunately, his job satisfaction came to an end just before the spring semester ended. He was caught blowing marijuana smoke into a collie's face.

He claimed, "I could have made that dog talk if I could have just got him high enough."

Later he confessed another of his crimes against dogkind. He had performed a controlled experiment on a group of puppies.

"Ya see, Eddie, this is what I did. I took one group, I called them Group A, and another group I called Group B. That way I wouldn't get confused."

"Very clever."

"Then I gave Group A a daily dose of weed. I didn't give nothin' to Group B. At the end of the month, Group A was all fucked up.

They couldn't walk a straight line. They kept bumpin' into walls and actin' weirder than shit."

"What happened to Group B?"

"They was okay," he paused pensively for a moment or two, and then said, "Jus' goes to show one thing, dude." He smiled like a sage. "That fuckin' weed is good shit!"

5

The Smartest Man in the World

Sam, in spite of himself, was doing very well since he lost his job at the kennel. He was now entitled to unemployment compensation. This was a stroke of dumb luck, and he took full advantage of the opportunity.

He would rise about ten o'clock, mosey on over to the park, and sometimes get lucky with a girl. Afterwards, he would play pool, eat dinner and smoke dope until midnight. This was great for him, at least for the time being.

Unfortunately, I had to endure the smartest man in the world, Winston Ashford Gonzales. Yes, I finally met the "Winston" that I had heard so much about since my arrival at Del Norte.

He was an arrogant, pretentious, pipe-smoking graduate student and the teacher's assistant in one of my English classes. He stood just about six feet, and his dark blond hair was shorter than that of most of the students, which automatically made him the focus of some suspicion. He always wore a tweed jacket with leather patches on the elbows, baggy pants and a stay-pressed shirt.

Like everyone else who had ever had him as a T.A., I immediately hated his guts. He acted as if he knew everything, and all the good-looking women squirmed and at times even squealed when he walked into the room.

To make matters worse, Winston took an immediate liking to me. This unnerved me for two reasons: One reason was that some of the guys in the class were convinced he was a homosexual, in spite of the rumor that he had sacked at least half the women on campus. The other reason was that I knew he had overheard me trying to talk Sally Bridgelet into writing my next paper for me, and I suspected I was about to be reprimanded for it.

"Let's grab a cup of espresso over at the student union," he said to me one day after class. "Your treat."

Sheepishly, I complied. I didn't want to go, but I didn't want to offend him either. He was, after all, the teacher.

"Delano," said Winston, sipping his espresso. "That's a curious name. Hispanic?"

I hated to admit it. I was afraid he would hold it against me. I shrugged my shoulders and nodded my head.

"We Hispanics have to stick together," he said to my surprise. Winston Ashford Gonzales was about as Hispanic as Lord Chesterfield.

By mere accident of genealogy, I was born with a Spanish sur-name, but I would have just as soon changed it to Smith or Jones. No one had ever thought of me as a Mexican. Because of my eyes and my skin complexion, people often mistook me for Italian, or French, which was fine with me considering how badly Mexicans were treated in this so-called egalitarian society.

A Chicano activist once accused me of being ashamed of my race. This was not true. I simply didn't know much about my race, nor did I really care to learn anything about it.

Of course, I respected the Aztecs. They built pyramids or some-thing. And at the Alamo, the Mexicans really gave it to Davy Crock-ett. So viva Mexico. But so what? That was a long time ago, and I had nothing to do with the building of pyramids or the outcome at the Alamo. I was born in Southern California, so was my father, and so was his.

Anyway, this Winston didn't strike me as the La Raza type.

"You don't look Hispanic." I didn't know why I said that. My curiosity must have got the best of me.

"One might say the same of you."

"But you don't act like one either. In fact you seem more Anglo than most Anglos."

"Very observant, Delano. If you're going to succeed in this Anglo-Saxon Disneyland, you're going to have to out-Gringo the Gringos." He had the look of a sage who was pleased that he had just farted. "So how long have you been a student at Del Norte, Ed?"

"A little over a year. I'm a sophomore."

Silence passed between us as we sat in a quiet corner of the café overlooking an artificial pond surrounded by Astroturf.

35

What he said next affirmed my earlier fear.

"Well, I didn't just ask you over here to chat. Let me get right to the point. I overheard you trying to talk Sally Bridgelet into writing your next paper. Shame on you."

"Well, I was kind of rushed," I stammered, "and I've never done it before."

"I knew a poor fool once who talked a girl into writing a paper for him, and he ended up married to the bitch. He's teaching in a public school now. That's what he deserves. But you seem like a bright enough fellow. Why'd you do it?"

"I've been swamped," I lied.

"You know, Ed. That last paper you wrote on seafood in American literature was clever. It must have taken a great deal of time, no?"

"It did. It was against my better judgment, but I felt obliged to put some effort into it. And I don't mind telling you—I was very disappointed with the B you gave it."

"Well, Ed, you *are* a B student."

He studied me for a moment to see my reaction. Though I didn't show it, I was seething.

"It's not that you couldn't be an A student," said Winston. "You have, I suspect, tremendous potential."

"I do?" I asked, more from surprise than curiosity.

"Why, yes, of course you do. In fact, if my instincts are correct, I suspect that you have exactly what it takes to be an A student at a school like Del Norte. We have much more in common than heritage. For a nominal fee, say fifty bucks a month, I can teach you how to succeed in college without doing any work at all. And you won't have to run the risk of ruining your life by getting married."

I was very suspicious of Winston Ashford Gonzales, but there was something fundamentally dishonest about him which I knew I could trust.

"Maybe we do have a lot in common. You say no work? I like that."

"Well, you have to work a little at making it look like you're working, but in actuality, you'll be doing very little. Believe me, every professor worth his salt practices this system. In fact, most successful executives, politicians, and county employees practice these proven methods. And probably the entire nation of Argentina."

"What do I do?"

He made a gesture of rubbing his thumb in a circular motion against his two fingers, which meant "first the money, then we talk."

We drove to my bank, where I intended to withdraw fifty dollars from my savings. As I filled out the withdrawal form, Winston was looking over my shoulder.

"You're going to need a lot more money than that. Fifty for me and at least a hundred for yourself."

"That will leave me nearly broke."

"You'll triple your money in no time. First, we need to buy you a new attire. You need at least one tweed jacket with leather patches. Something like mine."

"That's going to be expensive."

"Hardly. We can scour the thrift shops and buy it second hand."

"Won't it look old and used?"

"No, in fact it will look worn and comfortable, and you'll feel comfortable wearing it, as if this is what you've worn for years."

We found a jacket in a Salvation Army store for fifteen dollars. Next we drove to a used bookstore.

"Okay, this next step is essential," he said as we walked directly to a large bin of *Cliffs Notes* and *Monarch Notes*. "Everything you might need to know for any of your classes will be found right here. From now on, this is where you do your research."

"But I've been reading all of the texts. Doesn't that give me the edge?" I asked, feeling I had been ripped off somehow.

"No, it doesn't. In fact it distracts you from your real goal."

"My real goal?"

"Yes. Avoiding work. Besides, if you read the text on your own, you might come up with an original idea. And you wouldn't want that."

"I wouldn't? My professors are always begging for original ideas."

"Please," he said with a note of annoyance in his voice. "What they really want is to hear what they already know. You have to understand how much time they've invested into some of these picayune issues, how thoroughly they've studied them. You come along with an original thought and they have no idea of what to make of you. You become a threat." He composed himself. "Remember, they have the grade book."

"So I don't have to buy the texts, then. That'll save me a lot of money."

"Sorry, you do have to buy the books. Appearance is everything. After all, you can't be seen quoting from the *Cliffs Notes*. You have to have the texts. But, you can buy them here used. Look for the ones with lots of markings, dog-eared pages and asterisks. It will look like you've really done a lot of reading. That will impress your professors. They will believe either that you actually read the text, which no one really does, or that you're very clever."

"Great. Then I can still sell them back to the bookstore afterwards."

"Good God, no! You put them on your bookshelf. In time you'll have your own literary library, and whenever you get a girl into your apartment, she immediately thinks you're some kind of poet and jumps into bed with you. It's much better than having an expensive stereo or sports car. Believe me."

"Okay. So no more long days and nights in the library, right?"

"Not entirely, Ed. You'll have to make an occasional appearance at the library to be seen by your professors. After all, they're obligated to do the same thing. Oh yes, in order to make the competition sweat, check out as many resource books as possible. Don't bother to read them. Just keep them until the end of the semester. It will count in your favor when the professor learns that it was you who had them."

"Is that it?" I said without hiding my disappointment. I was hoping for a little more for my money.

"No, we've only just begun. But for now you'll need just one more thing—a pipe."

"But I don't smoke."

"Neither do I, but you never see me without one. Nothing too elaborate. Something conservative will do. Remember, this is America. Appearance is everything."

I wrote off the fifty bucks I gave to Winston. I figured it would at least win me some favor in his class. As for the clothes, books and study guides, I needed them anyway. The pipe seemed useless, but I carried it around with me all the same.

What surprised me was that it didn't take long for my grades to improve. In fact, they were already rapidly moving upwards during the first month of his tutelage. Appearance *was* everything.

In the second month Winston asked, "Are you ready for lesson two?"

"Yes, as a matter of fact I am. Your tips have been fabulous."

"Of course they are. Now lesson two is a little late for this semester but it will come in handy next semester and even for graduate school. This is it: Never speak in the first two or three weeks of any seminar or class that requires discussion. Remember, it is better to be silent and thought a fool than to open your mouth and remove all doubt. I found that one in a Chinese fortune cookie."

"But if the grade is partially based on discussion, won't I lose my edge?"

"No. In fact, in those first few weeks the professor is just trying to figure out who's full of shit and who isn't. Just take notes the first few weeks. Not actual notes. Just observe the way the professor speaks. His physical gestures. Learn to imitate him. Write down key phrases that he repeats. Later you'll use these phrases as if you were quoting an intelligent source. He'll be flattered and think you're smart. Write down the comments other students make that he likes. Later you can repeat those observations and take full credit for them. Also, write down the negative comments he has for those he disagrees with, and make certain you never repeat them unless you're trying to discredit someone. They're the comments he uses to discredit the poor fools who actually read the text and have original ideas."

"This is insightful," I said as I took notes.

"Above all," he added, "be pretentious. Use words like 'hardly' and 'of course' with a biting edge in your voice, as if you had utter contempt for the person you're putting down. That always goes over well with the humanities crowd."

He smiled, placed his pipe in the corner of his mouth, and leaned back in his chair.

"Why don't you try it, Ed. Repeat after me. *Hardly.*"

"Hardly."

"No, you sound ill. Say it again."

"Hardly."

"Now you sound like a queer. It's easy to do that, but you don't want everyone to think you're queer, unless of course your professor is. You need to put a little less English into it. Say it again."

"*Hardly.*"

"Good! Manly, biting and erudite."

"Wow, I've been doing everything wrong since I started college. I can't believe it."

"I can. I've read your work. Remember this, as well: Never say anything that can be pinned down. Always say 'one might consider' or 'it would seem that' or 'you might say it appears' or some other such phrase. The second you commit yourself to a position, everyone will be on you like wolves, with the professor leading the pack. Oh yes, whenever you're about to speak, always act as if you are struggling with an idea. Give people the impression that you actually *think* about the things you say. You can't appear to be too perfect. That's why it's good to occasionally be self-effacing, but not too much or everyone will think you have an inferiority complex, and they'll hate you for it."

"Well, that's a lot to master in the next month."

"Yes, it is. I have a special lesson for you next time we meet. But first practice those I've already given you."

He rubbed his thumb in a circular motion against his fingers, and I paid him.

Everything continued to work beautifully. I was told by one of my professors that he'd never really noticed me until this past month.

"But your work has improved, Delano. Late bloomer, I guess."

Winston was a master. Of course, in class he was my English teacher and nothing more, but once a month he was my personal mentor.

The next time we met at the student union he began, "This month's lesson, Eddie, is going to make you money. You need more money."

"Yes, how'd you know?"

"You're a student. Besides, I saw your savings account, remember? What a disaster. What's your primary source of income?"

"The GI Bill, plus a small disability check from a wound I suffered."

"A disabled veteran! You're sitting on a gold mine, Delano. What kind of wound did you receive? Nothing too drastic?"

"My toe was shot off."

"Wonderful! Self-inflicted, I hope?"

"Yes, as a matter of fact it was. But please keep it to yourself. How'd you know?"

"I have a nose for talent, Delano. I knew you were special when I met you. Your secret is safe with me. Now let's play up this wound of yours. Can you limp a little?"

I limped away from our table and returned.

"Good, Ed," he said. "I see you've had practice. Now let's go over to financial aid and work up a sympathy angle. After all, you are also a member of the downtrodden Hispanic race," he added with a wink.

"Wait a second. There's a problem here. When I enrolled, I didn't think my grades were good enough to get in, so I told them I was black."

"That's even better! A black, Hispanic, disabled veteran. Delano! You've got it made. Why are you even in school? If you could only convince them you're a woman, a lesbian perhaps, they'd probably make you chancellor of the entire damn university!"

Winston was correct again. My first Basic Equal Opportunity Grant check came the next month. We were now working on a special scholarship that was meant to go specifically to South Sea Islanders. In the event that I had to make a personal appearance to pick up the check, Winston advised me to wear a woolly wig and rub shoe polish all over myself.

"If anyone questions you, try to eat them. They'll think you're a cannibal and leave you alone."

It sounded pretty stupid to me, but I said nothing.

Occasionally, he would pay me a visit at my bungalow. When he did, he made it out as if it were some kind of big deal, because he never socialized with his *protégés*. But he would show up anywhere he could get a free beer.

His first reaction to meeting Sam, my roommate, was negative. Sam mournfully explained his plight in his stoned, nasal accent.

"I gotta go find a job. It really sucks the big one. Know what I mean? My unemployment is almost over. I might have to go back to San Berdoo."

"My God!" Winston exclaimed after Sam left. "He must be the dumbest man alive. But this is good, Ed. Don't dump him. You need a dumb roommate for two reasons: One is that you can easily cheat him out of his possessions, and he'll never know it. The other is that you want girls to think you're kind and tolerant."

Suddenly, another vision passed through Winston's demented mind.

"Have you taken anthropology, Ed?"

"Yes, I have. Why do you ask?"

"Sam, of course. I just thought that if you hadn't taken anthro yet, you could use him as a project."

He stood up for a moment and made a gesture with his hands as if he were reading a newspaper.

"Del Norte student finds missing link!" He opened his hands and, with a polite smirk, added, "But, since you've already taken anthro, it's not relevant. Still, Sam is a valuable asset. You have good instincts, Ed."

By the seventh month, Winston had shown me where to buy good term papers and taught me how to fake Latin. He had also given me an in-depth explanation as to why one should never sleep with any female student who was sleeping with the professor.

This last lesson was not an easy one to accept. It seemed to be in direct conflict with my one-percent theory. But I didn't argue the point. His instruction had shown excellent results. For the first time since entering college, I felt I had a handle on things. And I was now on the president's honor roll.

My tutoring had come to an end, and Winston gave me his parting advice.

"Ed, I've tutored scores of undergrads, and you might be one of the more complex. If you have one flaw, I suspect it would be that you have a sense of compassion. It's a product of these liberal times, and it does have a purpose to some extent. Girls seem to remove their underpants much faster these days for liberals than they do for conservatives. But mark my words: one day compassion will be a dirty word and the Republicans will be fashionable again. I'd remember that if I were you."

"If I need any help, will you be available next semester?"

"You won't need any help, Delano. In fact I could learn a few things from you. Besides there are other troubled undergraduates here who are in dire need of assistance. For now, good bye and good luck. Oh yes, you owe me fifty dollars."

6

The Payoff

At the beginning of the following semester, I'd occasionally see Winston on campus with a new pupil repeating "hardly" or with a beguiled coed about to negotiate sexual favors for a better grade in one of his classes. But I was essentially on my own. It was frightening at first, but soon I was reaping the rewards of my hard-earned training.

On the first day of class, I checked out of the library every reference book on Hawthorne and Melville for my ten o'clock class, and everything on the theory of tragedy for my two o'clock philosophy class. The following day I did the same for my other courses. My little bungalow was filled with reference books that no one would use during the semester.

I bought all my textbooks at the used bookstore Winston had recommended, and it cost me only a fraction of what it used to. I also bought all the *Cliffs Notes*, the *Monarch Notes* and several other study guides that covered the subjects I was enrolled in.

In each class I placed my dog-eared books in a direct visual line from where my professor sat, knowing that sooner or later he would note my worn texts and assume the wear and tear was due to my close reading. Or that I was clever.

As instructed by Winston the previous semester, I studied each of my professors closely for mannerisms and speech patterns that I could later employ. The more notes I took, the more it must have appeared to both my peers and my teachers that I was either a brilliant student or a complete fool, or, and possibly even more impressive, both.

The first opportunity to put my new methods to the test came in the third week of the semester in my Hawthorne/Melville class. I had taken good notes from Professor Doolittle. They included the following:

> – *Pretentious, arrogant, legs crossed and shifted seven times.*
> – *Says "bravo" when someone says the right thing.*
> – *Says "absolutely" as if he were having an orgasm when someone says something he agrees with.*
> – *Says "yes yes" with impatient tone in voice when annoyed with student.*
> – *Says "Oh come now" when disgusted.*
> – *Says "One must consider" just before making a point.*
> – *"To understand Hawthorne one must" four times.*
> – *"Let me put it in other words" eight times.*
> – *"Let me get right to the point" six times.*
> – *"Indeed" five times.*
> – *Chuckled about a silly joke he repeated twice this week.*
> – *Clears his throat to get attention.*
> – *Lifts head back and speculates before speaking.*

The class discussion was on *The Scarlet Letter*. Professor Doolittle's major thesis was that Hawthorne was attacking the Puritan doctrine, and several students were disagreeing with him. I saw my chance and took it.

I cleared my throat, in the same manner as Doolittle, crossed my legs slowly and deliberately, and, after I knew I had everyone's attention, lifted my head up and then back, and paused.

"One must consider the underlying implications of the effect Puritanism had on the masses."

I really had no idea what I was saying. I was simply repeating a collage of phrases I had collected in my notes. But it stopped the class. All eyes were on me.

"Could you clarify this further, Mr. Delano?" asked Doolittle.

45

"Yes, let me get right to the point. Hawthorne had it in for the Puritans."

"Absolutely!" said Doolittle.

The faces of a few of the students in the classroom grew ugly with suspicion. One of them, Jordan Hatch, countered.

"But if you read the text closely—"

"Of course!" I said, cutting him off.

Doolittle laughed.

I withdrew my pipe from the inside pocket of my tweed jacket, placed it in the corner of my mouth, turned my body sideways, and thrust my legs comfortably over the empty chair next to me.

"But how can you say for certain that Hawthorne was attacking the Puritans?" argued Hatch. "It seems to me he was—"

"Hardly!" I said, with the Winston Ashford Gonzales seal of approval.

"Bravo, Delano!" said Doolittle.

"Honestly, Delano," Hatch pleaded. "I haven't understood one word you've said."

"Yes, yes," said Doolittle. "But Delano does have a valid point."

"Which is?" asked Hatch.

"Which is what?" I asked of Hatch.

"Which is what? I'm asking you," said Hatch.

"Oh come now. You're beginning to repeat yourself," I said.

"But—"

"Absolutely!" said Doolittle, cutting Hatch off sharply. "Maybe you should do a little more research, Mr. Hatch." He paused. "Oh yes. That reminds me. I've been meaning to ask this class something very important. Several of you have approached me to complain that all of the outside sources for this course have been checked out of the library. Is there someone in this class who has them?"

"Of course, Professor Doolittle. I have them," I said as I placed my pipe back into my inside jacket pocket.

"Oh," he said, a note of surprise in his voice. "Well, I should have figured from your line of reasoning that you would have been the one to have all the research material. I'm glad to see it hasn't gone to waste. Good job, Delano."

"But sir," said Hatch. "How are the rest of us going to do our re-search papers if Delano has all the material?"

"Yes, yes." He cleared his throat. "Mr. Hatch, this is not high school. We do not take our students by the hand to help them solve their problems."

"But..." he sputtered before being cut off again.

"No buts, young man. You should follow Delano's example. You don't see *him* asking the professor for special favors. Obviously, he knows the art of literary research."

Several weeks later Winston approached me at the student union.

"I hear good things about you, Edward."

"Thank you. I really owe it all to you. I got an A on every paper I've turned in so far. In fact, Doolittle gave me an A on a paper I haven't yet turned in. That term paper service you turned me on to was a wonderful investment. I have them on a retainer."

"Good idea. Look, I'm going over to the antiwar demonstration today. I was wondering if you would like to join me."

"Antiwar demonstration? You? I thought you were against taking political stands."

"This has nothing to do with politics. There should be some good-looking women there carrying signs and screaming antiwar slogans. We might get lucky."

On our way to the demonstration, we passed a group of bald young people wearing yellow robes and chanting. I'd seen Baba Rama's people before, hustling small change from students.

"What's this all about, Winston?"

"Baba Rama? Now that's a real money maker he's onto." He seemed impressed. "Sends his followers out to panhandle for him. It's amazing. He's got these morons running around collecting untaxable income and he pays them absolutely nothing. You know, it's preachers like him who give religion a *good* name!" Then his eyes lit up. "Say, Ed, you have a certain quality that would serve you well in the religious field. Perhaps we could call you the Reverend Delano."

"I don't believe in God."

"Excellent! The best preachers never do. I can see you in a black suit and tie and speaking in tongues."

"I don't know, Winston. It would sort of cramp my life style. No drugs or women."

"Have *you* got a lot to learn!" he said disappointedly.

The sounds of the demonstration became louder. We were approaching a large group of students singing antiwar songs. I picked out a redhead from my Shakespeare class among the demonstrators.

"Look! Over there, Winston. There's Barbara McDoogle."

"Stay away from her, Eddie."

"She's smiling at me. I think she likes me."

"She's having an affair with Hatfield, your Shakespeare professor."

"That makes perfect sense. Now I understand. She said something absolutely ridiculous the other day in class and Hatfield enthusiastically agreed with her."

"What was it?" Winston asked with a smile.

"She said that Shakespeare was a European, as if it were some great discovery, and Hatfield replied that it was an excellent observation."

"See? These women get all the breaks. And they want to be our equals. It's incredible!"

"I can understand them wanting to be equal. But why do you suppose they're so angry, Winston?"

"I suppose they're upset that the government doesn't draft them the way they draft men and put them at risk of being either killed or permanently maimed for a cause that nobody is really clear about. Or perhaps it's because they've been excluded from certain professions. You rarely see women collecting garbage or working as gas station attendants, do you?"

"I think they're more concerned about getting an equal crack at law or medical school."

"Yes, but many men are also excluded from those professions, and you don't see them burning their jock straps. Besides, there are a lot of women who've done quite well for themselves marrying doctors and lawyers. Now what would happen to those women who were planning to marry a doctor or a lawyer if fewer men go into those professions?"

"But why are they so angry?"

"Who knows. If you ask them, they'll blame it on men like you and me. The whole thing is silly. Don't take them too seriously."

The crowd grew very large and a speaker was screaming something about the war.

"By the way, Ed. I've been meaning to ask you something. How are the grants coming along?"

"Good," I replied halfheartedly. "I've been receiving money from the Friends of the Disabled Fiji Veterans and from the Hispanic Foundation."

"You don't seem happy about it," he said with an inquisitive squint.

"I'm not happy. I feel very nervous about the whole thing. The other day I received another letter from the Black Student Union and I felt very guilty about what I've been doing."

"Guilt." He said it with disgust. "I thought you were above such trivial feelings. Don't let it sour your attitude."

"But I may have taken away someone else's opportunity to go to school."

"You're looking at it the wrong way, Edward. You see, these programs often go begging for recipients. If they don't find enough qualified students to take the money, the programs are often canceled. You are providing a very noble service, not only for our downtrodden Hispanic brothers, but for our fellow minorities in the African-American and the South Sea Islander communities."

"When you put it that way..." I considered his reasoning. "Well, I guess it's okay. But if they ever find out, they'll kick me out of college."

"Delano. Don't worry," he said reassuringly. "You've come far since I first met you, and you have so much natural talent. Don't blow it over something as ridiculous as guilt."

"I guess you're right. But I don't always like the way I feel about some of the things you've taught me."

"Like what, for instance?" he asked with a note of resentment in his voice.

"Well, I've been getting A's making a mockery of my professors and a lot of hardworking students. This guy, Jordon Hatch—"

"The man's an imbecile. He's in my world lit class."

"No, he's not an imbecile. He really works hard, and he's probably only earning C's."

"He's not your responsibility. Don't you think I've made the same offer to him that I made to you? He's a tightwad. He does have a good-looking girlfriend, though."

He paused for a moment as we were interrupted by loud applause for the speaker. When the applause died down, he said, "Excuse me, but I see Wanda Jennings over there. I'll see you around, Delano. You're on your own."

I watched Winston walk away through the crowd of students, chanting along with everyone else, "Hell no! We won't go!"

I wondered if I had made a mistake. Before beginning my apprenticeship with him, the lowest grade I had earned was a B-, and that was in his class. Sure, I'd earned a few more A's since using his "proven methods." But what was wrong with earning B's if I was learning something? Besides, some of his methods could get me expelled.

Or worse. If it were ever discovered how much money I was taking from all of these minority grants, they wouldn't just expel me—they'd put me in prison.

Still, life had become much easier since I met up with Winston. I had money in the bank, food in the cupboard, and the life style that I had set out to find when I enrolled here. I woke up late, ate what I wanted, went where I wanted, and did whatever I pleased. And still, I was getting A's.

And I owed it all to the wise teachings of my benefactor, Winston Ashford Gonzales. Maybe his teachings, as unorthodox as they seemed, were not so bad.

Except the one about not sleeping with any girl who was sleeping with the professor. A girl like Barbara McDoogle.

There she was again. She *would* have to be wearing shorts. I gazed at her long, shapely legs.

Our eyes met and she gave me a flirtatious smile.

How could I possibly listen to Winston?

50

7

Politics and Worms

Winston was right about not trying to save my fellow human beings from political folly, but not for the reasons he gave. It was not that I didn't care that the war was wrong, nor did I believe that all the protesting was meaningless. After all, who could argue in favor of war? It would be like arguing for racial injustice, or trying to justify world hunger.

But for me, the war was over—they couldn't draft me a second time. My concerns now were a little more practical, like getting into Barbara McDoogle's pants without Professor Hatfield finding out. And though I succeeded on that level, my success was to complicate my life in ways I was yet to understand.

Maybe it was my fault that things turned out the way they did. I knew I misled Barbara. But I wouldn't have gotten lucky if I hadn't given her the impression that I was more than just simply against the war.

Actually, she believed that I was some kind of agent of intrigue. She had this strange notion that I was out to save mankind through radical politics, that I was here on campus to assist the New People's Army.

Maybe it was because I told her so.

"I've come to assist some of the organizers behind the scenes here."

She filled in the blanks. After all, it made me look a lot more interesting than if she knew I only went to the antiwar rally to score on women. Little did I know that she, also, was making herself look a lot more interesting by embellishing my lie with further exaggerations. It seemed I was to be her claim to fame.

In the meantime, I was struggling over the plight of my fellow human beings in a different way, or with one human being in particular—Sam. If I was to be concerned with anyone, it would be him. He was running out of money, and if my calculations were correct, he soon wouldn't be able to pay his share of the rent. What made the matter urgent was that he did not have a grasp of the situation.

One day I found him on the back porch looking over an ad in a magazine.

"What's up, Sam? Find a job yet?"

"Gonna give this dude a call 'bout going into worm farming."

I must have had an incredulous expression on my face because Sam insisted on explaining the ins and outs of the worm industry.

"It's a golden opportunity. Financial freedom. Says so right here. See, what most people don't know is that worms breed like rabbits," he said, pointing to a line in the ad. "See, this is how it works: I buy a bunch of worms with a hundred bucks."

"Where are you going to get the money?" I asked, trying to hide my concern.

"We'll get to that part later. Ya see, these worms multiply rapidly. I sell half of them and keep half of them. They just keep reproducing, so I never run out. All I have to do is give 'em dirt and water. Hell, anyone can do that. I can do it right here in the back," he said, nodding to the small patch of earth we called our backyard.

"Have you thought this thing through, Sam? Who buys worms?"

"Other worm farmers."

"But how many worms do you have to sell in order to make it worth your while?"

He sighed and shook his head.

"Some people see limitations and others see possibilities. Eddie, I hate to say it, but you got a real negative outlook on life. Here I have the opportunity of a lifetime, and you act like I was some kind of fool. I was halfway tempted to ask you if you wanted to go into business with me."

I failed to see the connection between worms and rent money.

"Thanks for the thought, Sam. But I don't think I'd make much of a wormsman."

"You oughta think about it Eddie. I owe you one, and this would be my way of paying you back."

"I'm due back on planet Earth, Sam."

"Huh? Boy, sometimes you're weird," he said pensively.

It didn't take long for Sam to act upon his plan. Several days later, he greeted me as I returned from the market. He was finishing a doobie.

"I got my worms! Come with me. I'll show 'em to you."

Earlier he had constructed a wooden contraption, a large rectangular frame, in the backyard. It was now filled with dirt and worms. And the worms were everywhere, twisting and crawling into and around clumps of black earth.

Sam's joint was now no more than a roach. He examined it and ate it. Then he turned to me, smiling.

"The whole thing cost me a hundred and fifty bucks. Was the last of my unemployment check."

"What about the rent? You got money for the rent, right?"

"Hey, man. Lighten up. Give me some space, ace." Like a rebuffed adolescent, he continued, "Man, you don't see it. This is a fucking gold mine."

"But you don't have enough money to pay next month's rent."

"Hey, dude, it takes money to make money," he said, lighting another joint.

As I left for school that afternoon, I looked out the kitchen window and saw Sam watering his worms. He had a goofy, catatonic grin on his face. A large yellow joint dangled from the corner of his mouth.

The weather was unseasonably warm and clear, so I decided to save gas and parking fees and ride my bicycle.

I enjoyed the ride to school; I meditated as I pedaled. Then, as I approached the campus and the difficulty of pedaling increased in direct proportion to the rising incline of the road, I raised my head for a moment and saw a single black cloud in the distance. It was peculiar, as it stood out in direct contrast to the clear sky that surrounded it.

I returned my attention to the road. Ahead of me now I saw a crowd of students at the main entrance of the college. I remembered Barbara McDoogle mentioning that another antiwar rally was planned.

The protestors appeared to be waiting for someone. A cop was watching the protestors from a strategic distance.

I decided to avoid the entire scene by staying across the street from the campus and riding on past the main entrance to a smaller parking lot farther along. That way, also, I could park my bike closer to Dr. Stanton's classroom.

Suddenly, the brief burst of a siren caught my attention. A motorcycle cop pulled me over.

"What's the problem, officer?"

"Your reflector is broken."

He asked for my license and went to radio in my I.D. He returned with his gun drawn and read me my rights.

It seemed I had been a wanted man for several years and didn't know it. I had failed to appear for a ticket, the ticket I had received and torn up in a moment of defiance—and for the same broken bicycle reflector!

As a backup unit arrived to assist the motorcycle cop, the students at the main entrance began moving in my direction. They were cursing the cops.

Why they would be concerned was beyond me. Then it became clear. In the middle of the crowd was Barbara McDoogle. She must have thought that I was on my way to the campus to covertly help organize the protesters.

At the urging of an amplified, metallic voice, the curses from the crowd grew louder.

Just as I was handcuffed, a photographer snapped a picture, and a reporter from the local paper walked up to me and asked if I was with the Weathermen.

I didn't understand him. Who were the Weathermen?

Taking him literally, I looked at the sky and realized that the same black cloud I saw earlier was now hovering above us.

"It looks like rain to me," I replied.

"I take that as a yes," said the reporter with a cryptic smile.

The crowd grew nastier, and Barbara McDoogle shouted out.

"Don't take any shit from those fascist thugs, Eddie! They can't treat you like that! You've got your rights!"

Before I could reply, the cops did something unexpected. Perhaps it was panic: there were only two of them, and I did notice what looked like fear in their eyes.

But then maybe they had some other agenda and my arrest was

confounding the situation. Indeed, it was more than likely a quick gesture to placate the mob.

Whatever the reason, the arresting officer released me and returned my license.

"Beat it, kid."

I hopped on my bike and beat it out of there as fast as my legs could pedal. Behind me I heard the students cheering my release.

All kinds of thoughts raced through my head. If they were going to arrest me, they now knew where I was. But my driver's license still had my parents' address. And since they didn't actually bust me on the campus, they would not know for certain that I was a student at Del Norte.

Besides, were they actually going to send cops to the college to get me for a broken bicycle reflector?

In all the commotion, I missed the introduction to a riveting lecture on the role of freckles in *Huckleberry Finn*, an intellectual point Dr. Stanton felt was foolishly neglected by the dons of academia. He ground a few gears shifting onto a companion thesis about the number of times Twain used the word *the*.

"The word *the* should not be seen as merely an article. No, it plays a much larger role..."

As engaging as the idea was, I just couldn't concentrate. I feared that at any moment the Del Norte sheriff's deputies, the state police, and the FBI would rush into the classroom and arrest me for my broken bicycle reflector. My life was screwed!

On my way home, I cruised through the center of campus, where it seemed as if everyone knew me. A stranger walking with several cute girls blocked the bike path and greeted me.

"Say, man! You're the dude who got busted. Far out. We were all waiting to hear you speak out against the war." He reached out his hand and introduced himself, "I'm Richard."

"I think you've made a mistake," I said, as one of the girls, a pretty blonde, smiled coyly at me.

"It's cool man. You don't have to worry. I'm on your side," replied Richard. "Say, man, why don't you meet with me and my friends at Fernie's Hideaway?"

Figuring that the blonde was going to be there, I took Richard up on his offer. Maybe he had some kind of insight as to what had happened today. Maybe he could help make sense out of it all.

When I arrived at Fernie's, the blonde girl was not there. I would have left, but there were a number of other attractive girls in the place; moreover, they all acted as if they recognized me and they were greeting me with approving smiles.

Of course, I had been to Fernie's more than once. It was a gathering spot for those in the counterculture, where politicos planned the next revolution, folk singers sang about their personal changes and the girls they screwed over in order to make those changes, and feminists traded telephone numbers with women who looked like truck drivers. And today was no different.

Richard took me by the arm and introduced me to his friends. They were seated in the corner of the café beneath a row of hanging fern plants.

"Hey, Mike! Fred, Cheryl. This is that dude they busted at the riot. His name's Eddie."

Cheryl got my attention immediately. She was an attractive redhead wearing denim overalls.

"It really wasn't a riot, and I didn't actually get busted," I said, expecting their disappointment. It was safe to assume that somehow they had placed some significance to my broken bicycle reflector that was greatly exaggerated.

"We know, Eddie," said Mike as he reached for my hand and gave me the brother's handshake. "Barbara has already given me the lowdown on you."

Fred and Cheryl examined me, and Mike said, "Sit down, Ed."

Simultaneously, they gave Richard a chilling stare, which dismissed him as if he were no more than a lowly minion in their egalitarian cause. Richard stood nearby, leaning against the wall.

As I sat down, a waitress approached the table. She seemed to take an immediate disliking to us.

"Wha'da ya want?" she asked angrily.

"Espresso for all of us," said Mike with a note of authoritative rudeness in his voice that settled any disagreements.

Fred peered out at me over his wire-rimmed glasses.

"You see, Eddie," he said. "We're in the middle of something real big."

I imagined that I had just been spoken to by the next Lenin.

Mike leaned back into his chair, pushed aside his long dark hair and stroked his beard.

56

"That's right, Eddie. This is big stuff."

Perhaps he was the next Trotsky.

"What do you want from me?" I asked.

Then Cheryl angrily intruded, "Mike, Fred. Let's cut the crap!"

She looked at me and had no idea that I was mentally undressing her. She had creamy, delicious skin.

"Eddie," she said, "we're taking over the library."

"The library? The school library?"

Both Mike and Fred leaned forward.

"Not so loud, Eddie," Mike whispered. "Are you with us?"

"What's the point?" I replied in a whisper. "I mean, why? Why take over the library?"

They looked at each other in disbelief. It was incomprehensible to them that anyone would question their plans.

Then, as if he were explaining the obvious to a three-year-old child, Fred broke the silence.

"Man, because we're protesting third-world exploitation!"

"I'm sorry. I didn't know. What are you going to do?"

"We're going to rename it," said Cheryl. Her beautiful almond-shaped green eyes flared in anger beneath her bright red hair. "We're going to call it the Idi Amin Solidarity Library!"

"But what do you want with me?"

"We need someone with experience, and who's not afraid of going to jail for what he believes in," replied Cheryl.

I was still undressing her when Mike, or Fred, said, "Well, Eddie? Are you with us?"

The three of them now had my undivided attention. They leaned forward, anticipating my answer.

"I think you've got the wrong person," I replied. "I'm not who you think I am."

"Who are you, then?" asked Mike, a furious expression twisting his face.

"I'm just a student," I said simply.

They looked at each other questioningly, then at me.

"Personally, I don't give a rat's ass what you call the library," I added. "Besides, isn't Idi Amin a cannibal or something?"

I immediately regretted my words when a look of disgust and then anger clouded over Cheryl's pretty face. I mentally put her clothes back on and stood up to leave.

"You fucking pig!" she screamed.

The folk singer singing about his changes and the girl he screwed over stopped. The feminists exchanging phone numbers with women who looked like truck drivers stopped. The lazy waitress who took an immediate disliking to us stopped. All eyes were focused on me.

Self-consciously and quickly, I exited Fernie's Hideaway.

Mike must have followed me out the door. I was halfway down the street before he caught up with me.

"Very good, Delano. You know how to play it cool. Your secret is safe with me."

"Honestly, Mike. I'm not what or who you think I am."

"Excellent," he said with a conspiratorial wink.

I returned home at dusk and found Sam standing where I had last seen him, in the backyard. I called to him, and when he entered the kitchen, I saw a look of horror on his face.

"They're all dead," he said.

"Who's dead?"

"The worms. They're all dead. I guess I lost track of time. I kept on watering them. I really don't know how long I was doing it. I was kinda stoned. I kept thinking over and over about how I finally found my calling in life."

I didn't really want to know any more, but Sam continued.

"You see, I was counting my money—just like that old saying, 'Don't count your eggs until they're hatched'. I was smoking one doobie after another, just thinking 'bout getting all that money, and just for watering worms. I was way out there, man..."

He had a faraway gaze on his face. Then he realized he was elsewhere.

"Anyways," he continued, "all of a sudden it dawned on me. I'd been standing in the same place for a long time. I realized just then that I had washed away all of the earth from the worm pen."

His jaw lowered as he recalled the image.

"I could see all these worms floating all over the place. Most of them was bloated up and had changed colors. They didn't look too healthy. A lot of them were out in the driveway. And then Mr. Rafferty drove up the driveway. He squashed most of them. Insult to injury."

He sighed, resignedly. I said nothing.

"Must be karma, Eddie."

Sam's forlorn face was transformed by a startling noise. Some-one was banging on the front door. Mechanically, Sam went to an-swer it.

"Hey Eddie," he said, returning. "That phony friend of yours is here. You know, Mr. Know-It-All."

Winston Ashford Gonzales entered the kitchen, scrunching up his nose as if offended by Sam's body odor. Sam left, despondently.

"Have you seen this?" Winston asked, producing the local news-paper.

It had a photograph of me with a caption below it that read: "Radical Evades Capture."

"That's a pretty lousy picture," I said, realizing that no one who looked at it, aside from Winston, would recognize me.

I read the ensuing article, and to my relief, they'd screwed up my name, as well:

> Radical activist, Edmond Delamo, evades
> police under a cloud of confusion at today's
> protest rally. Though police refuse to com-
> ment, a reliable source claims Delamo was
> at Del Norte today to help rally organizers
> from behind the scenes and is a prime sus-
> pect in a number of terrorist activities.

"Delano, how could you? You were my star pupil!" said Winston.

"Relax. It was a mistake. Besides, no one will recognize me from that picture, and they screwed up my name."

"Mistakes like this can ruin you. Never take political sides—un-less you can show a quick profit from doing so."

"I had nothing to do with the protest rally. I just happened to be at the wrong place at the wrong time."

"I want you to look very closely at the other photograph. Do you see that face?" he asked, pointing to one of the protestors. It was Mike from Fernie's. "Whatever you do, stay away from him and his friends."

"Tell me something I don't know."

"Okay, I will. He's the leader of the New People's Army."

"Well, that explains a lot," I said somberly.

"I figured it would." There was a long, Winston Ashford Gonzales pause before he added, "Well, Delano. How are you going to worm your way out of this?"

From the other room, Sam groaned.

8

San Berdoo

In his drive for success, Sam had been highly motivated by the fear of failure, which for him meant a one-way ticket back to San Bernardino. According to him, going back meant he'd have to eat more crow than he could bear.

His parents and friends had told him that he was a fool for going off to school and leading the life of a flower child. His father, on more than one occasion, had suggested that Sam could always pump gas for a living. His father told him that working at the old family-owned gas station had been good enough for him and his father, and he couldn't see why it wasn't good enough for Sam.

But Sam wanted to see the world, and Del Norte was just his first stop. Dropping out of school didn't bother him, nor did getting fired from the kennel. The fact he had got the job at the kennel in the first place was proof enough that he had a chance of breaking away from that old gas station.

However, the failure of the worm farm almost had him packing his bags. For days he collected the few survivors of his flooded mini-plantation and tried to start it up all over again. Nevertheless, he finally came to his end.

But Sam was stubborn. I found him one morning reading a magazine, the same one that had prompted his interest in worm farming.

"Hey Eddie, check this out. It's an ad for a job stuffing envelopes. You can make from two to six hundred dollars a week."

I took the magazine from his hand and stared at a picture of a moronic, smiling woman with a caption that read: "I earn big bucks in the comfort of my own home, and it really works!"

"I'm gonna check it out," said Sam.

61

"Aw, man!" I tossed the magazine down and pointed at the ad accusingly. "I don't mean to disillusion you, but that's got to be some kind of a scam. If *anyone* could make six hundred dollars a week just stuffing envelopes, *everybody* would be doing it."

"You know, Eddie," he looked at me critically. "I like you and I still owe you one, but you always see the pessimistic side to things. Come on," he pleaded. "Think positive!"

No one wanted Sam to be successful more than I did, but I remained skeptical.

"What about the worm farming, Sam?"

The memory gave him pause.

"Well, it coulda worked out, maybe," he said dejectedly.

Then a peculiar look crossed his face. I realized a new thought was taking place. I could tell he was having an idea because he looked as if he were constipated.

"Maybe you're right, Eddie. Maybe I'm going about this all wrong. How about this: we get a bunch of pictures made of me on crutches, with bandages wrapped around my face, and my arm in a sling. We take all those big mayonnaise and pickle jars Mrs. Rafferty keeps in the back and we put my picture on them. You can type up something that says, like, 'Support the Samuel T. Oswald Charity'. Then we put the jars all over town, and people put money in them."

He waited for me to make a comment.

I was bewildered. It sounded like an idea Winston would have thought up, not Sam.

I paused for a moment longer, then countered cautiously, "I don't know, Sam. It's a pretty good idea, but I think people might steal your money."

"You know, you're right. The whole thing is dishonest." He gathered himself. "Well, I gotta figure something out. I don't want to go back to San Berdoo."

That evening while I was studying in the kitchen, Sam interrupted me.

"Eddie!" he said excitedly. "Have I got a plan! It can make us big bucks!"

"I hope it's not stuffing envelopes. Or raising worms."

"No way," he laughed. "It has nothing to do with worms."

He opened the refrigerator and took out a can of beer.

"I met this dude named Hog, cause he loves bikes so much. He's

62

a real cool guy." He opened the can of beer and took a swig. "He's a biker. A big guy. Kinda dirty looking, but you can't judge a book by its cover, right?"

He paused to chug at his beer.

"Anyways, I was in this bar, kinda feeling low 'cause of the worms and stuff. And that's when Hog and his friends showed up. And I met a girl, too, but I'll tell you 'bout her later. Real high class."

"A high-class girl? In a biker bar?"

"Yeah, good-looking, too. Almost got it on with her right there on the pool table."

He paused again, recalling the girl.

"Anyways, Hog sees me and sees that I was real low, and he says, 'Cheer up, man. It can't be that bad!' And so I tell him how everything's been going wrong in my life, and I say I don't wanna end up back in San Berdoo. The minute I said San Berdoo, his eyes lit up. He says, 'San Berdoo? I'm from San Berdoo, too!'"

"Small world, Sam," I interjected.

"Eddie, that's exactly what I said. You know what? He even knows my grandpa's gas station. Anyways, he made me an offer on selling some high-grade weed! Some real righteous shit. I mean, I got some money left, and I'm gonna sell my stereo, my guitar, and my red lizard cowboy boots." He looked at me. "You in, Eddie?"

"No thanks. And whatever money you have left should be going to the rent, not to Hog."

"But this Hog dude has his shit together. We can make some *real* money."

"Look, I don't want to get involved with drugs and bikers. I don't think they mix too well."

"All right. You don't have to get superior and all. Just because you're a college man, don't go thinking you're too good, Eddie. Besides, if you ask me, I think you read too much."

"Read too much?" I thought I only read what I had to.

"Yeah, all those books you got piled up in your room. They'll screw you up. I knew this guy once. He read all the time. Had a ton of books just like you. Well, he got a brain tumor."

"Sam, please," I begged, hoping he would stop talking.

"No, really. He got a brain tumor and died, all because he read too much. I haven't touched a book since then. I get my learning from life."

I lowered my head slightly and raised my eyebrows. It must have been another incredulous expression to him.

He continued, explaining, "See, I seek out people with more experience than me. They become, like, my teachers. Like Hog. Hog says to me, 'There's two kinds of people in this world, Sam—the fuckees and the fuckors!'"

"Which one are you, Sam?"

He looked puzzled for a moment.

"Boy, Eddie. Putting it that way kinda makes you think."

I was not about to dwell on Sam's lack of common sense and money. Especially when there was a new girl two bungalows down the drive. She was very pretty. She had big, round blue eyes, honey-blonde hair and long wrap-around legs.

Unfortunately, Sam saw her first and claimed dibs. He announced his intention one afternoon as we sat on the porch drinking beer.

"Today's the day, dude," he said confidently.

It was done in the subtle tradition of the great lovers like Casanova or Don Juan. As she was leaving her bungalow, he puffed up his chest and strutted off the porch. Standing directly in front of her, he blocked her path and tossed back his mane of hair. He spoke in a deep voice reminiscent of Elvis Presley.

"Say, wild thang. You wanna smoke a doobie?"

She ran back to her bungalow as fast as she could and disappeared inside. Sam returned to the porch dejected.

"All I did was ask her if she wanted to smoke a doobie. She acted like I was some kind of pervert," he said and retreated inside.

A few minutes later she peeked out her door, surveyed the courtyard, and ventured forth once again. She walked quickly and self-consciously, but then her eyes caught mine and she slowed her pace. We exchanged bashful glances.

And it hit me. I could not describe it, but I felt weak and helpless. It was hard not to stare at her.

As she walked away, I regained control of myself, but for the rest of the afternoon and way into the night, I thought about her.

The following day I made certain not to miss the opportunity to meet her. I waited on the porch until she finally appeared at the corner.

Again walking with that same quick, self-conscious pace, she approached. As she neared me, we made eye contact and I smiled. She slowed down, but looked away nervously, as if she were in conflict as to what she wanted to do. Then she stopped and looked up at me and smiled. After a moment of awkward silence, we introduced ourselves.

Her name was Alice. She said that she'd seen me before at the college, and I told her she looked familiar as well.

A few more moments of silence passed between us, and I was beginning to feel uncomfortable.

"So," I said. "What are you studying?"

"I'm not really into traditional learning." Another moment of silence, and then she added, "I'm here to grow spiritually and artistically."

"What do you mean spiritually?" I asked, fearing she might be a born-again bigot.

"Spiritually—my inner self. I meditate and chant."

"That's real interesting," I said with the enthusiasm that comes from relief.

"I read auras, too."

I didn't say anything, fearing I'd reveal my ignorance of auras. I assumed she was talking about some kind of textbook.

"I get good vibes from you. You have a gentle aura."

"Thanks. You have a nice aura, too." Whatever the hell that was.

I looked into her eyes and was lost, and so, I felt, was she. I did not want to leave her for one moment. I wasn't sure what we talked about from that point on, but eventually the conversation meandered towards an unexpected question.

"What are you doing for dinner?"

Did she ask it, or did I? Did it matter?

I brought a bottle of wine. Alice had cooked something that looked awful, but I figured that if I wanted to get laid, I had to pretend it was edible.

"Looks great! Can hardly wait to eat. What's that chunky white stuff?"

"It's Japanese. It's called tofu."

"Tofu? What's it made of? It's not, like, mashed cows' eyes and chicken gizzards, is it?"

"No, it's meatless. It comes from soybeans."

"Soybeans?"

"Yes. I got this recipe at a retreat I attended last summer," she said, pointing to a flyer attached to her cupboard door. The photo on it was of Baba Rama—smiling, bearded, fat, and wearing a yellow muumuu. "I consider him to be the wisest person I've ever met."

"Really?" I said, reaching for the wine.

As I poured the wine, she lit a cigarette, smiled and said, "I'm a vegetarian. Well, kind of a vegetarian. I eat a little chicken and fish. But only every other day or so."

"I'm a meatatarian. I eat mainly animals. But only when I'm hungry."

She looked at me suspiciously as she took a long drag from her cigarette, but she wasn't bothered. She exhaled a stream of smoke and asked, "What's your major?"

"Liberal Arts. I'm thinking about going into teaching."

"That sounds very idealistic. What inspired you?"

"Well," I said as I stretched. "Three months off in the summer, Christmas vacation, Easter break, and a relatively light work load."

"I bet you'd be a great teacher," she said, grinding out her cigarette. "When do you graduate?"

"I'll finish up my B.A. at the end of next spring."

"Have you ever heard of polarity massage?"

I nodded no.

"You'll love it. Take off your shirt."

"I can do that."

The one-percent theory was still working.

When I returned home, Sam was sitting in the kitchen studying a map of Humbolt County. He lifted his eyes accusingly and said, "So how'd it go with the fox? Get any mud on your turtle?"

"Yeah, but I'm a bit confused about her."

"What's so confusing? She looks pretty good, if you ask me."

"Well, she's pretty good-looking and all, but she's got her head screwed on backwards. She's a vegetarian, which isn't so bad, but she made me eat some tasteless stuff called tofu. Then, after we got it on, she lit up a cigarette and started to chant gibberish. I was so confused, and I could hardly breathe. The cigarette smoke was making me sick."

"Yeah, man, but she's got a fine ass."

"Yes, that she does have," I said, realizing that maybe I should be more open-minded about soybeans, tobacco and gibberish.

"She looks like a pretty good catch if you ask me. But hey, I'm just a dumb shit."

He was right and I knew it. He was a dumb shit, and Alice was very special, but I felt I just couldn't get into a heavy relationship thing.

Then I realized I was lying to myself. Of course I wanted Alice. But I was afraid she might be like Debbie from my philosophy class. If I showed any concern for her, she would dump me.

"Eddie, I don't want to change the subject," he yawned, "but I've got some real heavy business I gotta take care of in the morning." He stood up and stretched. "If all goes well, I'll be rich."

"Good luck," I said.

"Luck has nothing to do with this." He pointed to his head. "It's brains. I offered you a chance to make some big bucks, but you thought you were too good. Well, don't say I didn't tell you so."

The following afternoon I found a note on the kitchen table:

> *Eddie,*
> *Having a little problem. I got to get out*
> *of town. If Hog shows up, tell him I'll pay*
> *him real soon. I'm good for the money.*
> *Maybe you was right. Sorry for the trouble.*
> *I'll be back as soon as the dust settles.*
> *Sam*

Moments after reading the note, a massive subhuman creature with obvious asshole tendencies appeared at my front door. He had long, mangy hair, a scruffy lice-infected beard, and a variety of blackhead pimples covering his face.

"Is there a tall moron with long hair named Sam here?"

"He left this morning."

"Where'd he go?"

"I don't know."

I handed him the note that Sam had left on the kitchen table. He examined it with squinted eyes.

"That fucking shit-head's gonna die!" He looked at me and said, "You don't know where he went, do you?"

"No, and I don't really care."

He grabbed me by my collar.

"You wouldn't be shitting me, would you, fuck-head?"

"I don't have the slightest idea where he may have gone!" I thought for a moment, then added, "Maybe Mexico!"

He released me and said, "If you're hidin' him, you're gonna die too!"

"Hey, lighten up. He's just my roommate. But if he comes back, I might kill him for you."

"He burn you too?"

"No. But I don't like the company he keeps."

"Well, I'm sorry about that. But the fucking dude ripped me off. And I trusted that fucker. Shit, I thought just because he was from San Berdoo, I could count on him."

Then his face lit up.

"That's it!" he exclaimed. "San Berdoo!"

He stormed out the door in a rush.

I was relieved that he didn't ask for my opinion. I really didn't know where Sam had gone, but I knew it wasn't San Berdoo.

9

Aurora Borealis

Two Months Later:

"Your aura is extremely negative Eddie," Alice observed. "You've been eating meat," she said, and then lit a cigarette.

"Not really. It was a hot dog."

"A hot dog! Do you realize what's in hot dogs?"

"Please don't tell me. I'm sure it's bad."

"Eddie, if only you would come with me and meet Baba Rama. He can teach you the joys of vegetarianism and the secrets of the universe."

"Wasn't Hitler a vegetarian?" I countered. She blew smoke in my face and I coughed. "I think we could both use a massage," I suggested sheepishly.

"You only like massages because we always end up having sex."

"What's wrong with that? It's good for our auras."

"You just want sex. That's all."

"If I go to hear Baba Rama, will you change your mind?"

"I don't think we should see each other for a while."

The truth of the matter remained that Alice confused me. She was fun to be with when she was not chanting, which she did all too often. The motor trips to the beach, bicycle excursions through the woods and long conversations that lasted into the early mornings were, inevitably, punctuated by her chanting. Not to mention her constant reminders about my barbaric eating habits.

Then, sometimes, her innocent idealism charmed me.

But a darker truth might have ended our relationship much sooner. I was having a lucky streak with other women. There was the one I met at the student union, the one I met in a bar across the street from the campus, and the one in my music appreciation class.

69

It was time to reassess my one-percent theory. Why was it that I was getting all these possibilities when I wasn't even trying? Could it be that that was the way it really worked?

Possibly there was something more to the formula than playing the odds. Maybe being with Alice gave me something other women found appealing. I felt I needed further research in order to figure it out. I needed a different test subject.

The one who came to mind was Ashley. She was in my morning class—Romance of the American Outlaw. Occasionally we made eye contact in a way that suggested to me that perhaps something more could be possible.

She was a delicate-looking woman. Her brown eyes made for an interesting contrast to her blonde hair, and her mouth was sensual in a way that made me want to close it with a kiss.

It didn't take long to learn her routine. After class she would normally go to the library. I figured that would be a good place to run into her.

Actually, I backed into her.

"Excuse me," I said. "I'm so clumsy." Then, with a feigned look of surprise, "Oh! I know you. You're in one of my classes, aren't you?"

She had a look of sudden recognition.

"Yes. American Outlaws. You sit on the right side of the room."

She'd noticed. A good sign, I thought. And she even knew exactly where I sat.

"Are you doing research here?"

"Yeah," she said with a disappointed sigh. "I have to finish this paper by next Tuesday."

"Maybe I can help," I said to her approving smile.

With a little calculation, one thing naturally progressed to another—small talk over coffee, walking to class together, exchanging telephone numbers.

I learned that her last name was Lychcraft—Ashley Lychcraft of the Newark Lychcrafts. I also learned that she had recently broken up with her boyfriend. A stroke of luck. Girls this good-looking usually came equipped with boyfriends.

She was a couple of years older than I and a returning graduate student. She had been a teacher the previous year. Then, claiming some stress-related ailment, she had filed for disability and created for herself a new career: writing grants for special education projects. How the grants actually worked never became clear to me.

One morning after class she told me about her most recent coup, a proposal for teaching deaf children how to play the piano. When she said this, I facetiously made a suggestion.

"Why don't you teach blind kids how to paint?"

Not detecting my sarcasm, her eyes lit up like two bursting firecrackers, and at that moment I knew it would only be a matter of time before I could charm her out of her pants.

"That's a wonderful idea, Eddie!" She considered a moment. "Why don't you come over to my place and we can toss a few ideas back and forth."

We set a date for later in the afternoon. In the meantime, I returned home for my midday nap.

I was greeted by Alice. Guilt almost knocked me off my feet when I saw her in tears. She stood at my door, blocking my entrance.

"Eddie, did Mr. Rafferty give you one of these?"

She handed me a letter:

> *Dear Tenant,*
> *I'm pleased to inform you that I have sold the bungalows to a developer for a sizable sum of money. The Mrs. and myself intend to go to Hawaii to continue our retirement. I realize this is short notice, but consider yourself evicted. You have until the end of May to pack your belongings and leave.*
>
> > *Aloha,*
> > *Huxley Rafferty*

"What am I going to do, Eddie?" She looked crestfallen. "Do you have plans? Maybe I can live with you."

For just a moment, I liked the idea. But then I imagined us shopping in some wacko health-food store for tofu hot dogs. And I thought about all the chanting and the talk about auras. And then I thought about Ashley.

"This is no time to panic, Ash..." I caught myself just in time, "Alice."

71

"It's pretty hard to find a place to live around here, ya know," she said. "Do you realize we gotta be out of here a week after final exams?"

"My buddy Winston used to run a housing racket. Something will work out," I said.

"I know what *I'm* going to do," she said in a moment of sudden elucidation. "I'm going to see Baba Rama."

"Alice, I'd think it over if I were you. That guy's running some kind of scam."

"Do you know what your problem is? You don't trust anybody. Baba Rama doesn't have a wicked bone in his body."

"That's because he's made out of blubber."

"At least he doesn't eat *hot dogs*. I'm sure I can find a place with him. He told me he has room on his ranch for all of his children."

She lit a cigarette and scurried off to the pay phone at the corner.

I was glad to see her leave. I feared she would continue to suggest that we live together, and it was better to avoid any negative confrontations with her. Moreover, I knew that under pressure I might give in to her suggestions.

After my nap, I drove across town to Ashley's. She was one of the lucky students. She had rented a small farm outside of town. Part of her income came from boarding horses.

I stood on her back porch and watched her lead her prize beast, a palomino mare, through the corral gate. As she approached, I realized I was really taken by her. I could see myself strolling across an open field holding hands with her. The mental image evoked a warm, fuzzy feeling in me.

"Come on down and get acquainted," she said. "She won't bite."

"That's okay. I'll stay right here on the porch."

"She's very gentle."

"Yes, but I didn't realize horses were so big."

She reacted with a disappointed smirk, so I reluctantly stepped down off the porch, stumbled, and limped forward. The horse was huge.

"You say they don't eat people?" I asked.

"They don't even nibble. Go ahead and pet her."

As I stroked her, Ashley looked at my leg.

"I hope you don't mind me asking, but is there something wrong with your leg?"

72

I assumed there was an absence of color in my face that made her think I was embarrassed by her question. Little did she know that I was terrified by the horse.

"I'm sorry, I didn't mean to pry. It's just that you bear some resemblance to Byron."

"Brian who?"

My mind was on the horse. It looked hungry to me.

"*Byron*—the poet," she said, a note of disbelief in her voice. "Look, I'm sorry. I should never have brought it up."

"The limp comes and goes," I said. "I guess I shouldn't be so self-conscious."

"I won't bring it up again."

"Well, it's not my leg. It's a missing toe."

"How did it happen?"

"I really don't like talking about it," I said, hoping to add a degree of mystery to my persona.

Her face turned red as she tried to regain her poise.

"I'm sorry. I really didn't mean to pry. But you do bear a resemblance to Byron."

The ensuing silence fed her curiosity like dry wood feeds a fire.

"Was it an accident? You're toe?"

"Naw." I shoved my hands into my pockets and modestly added, "Lost it in Nam."

"You were in the army?" She asked it in a way that suggested she was impressed.

"Yeah, but let's drop it. I'm not really ready to talk about it."

She looked at me with wide-eyed interest. It didn't matter that the war was unpopular. It didn't matter that most people would spit on a veteran. What mattered was that I had a mysterious past. I had said just enough to hook her.

We led the horse to the corral and then strolled quietly back across the yard. Her mood seemed to shift to one of preoccupation. When we got to the porch, I asked, "Is there something wrong?"

"Oh, it's nothing. I was thinking about my ex-roommate. She met this guy and moved in with him."

"You need a roommate?" I reached for the eviction notice I had placed in my pocket earlier that day. "I need a place to stay."

"I don't know if that's a good idea," she said, brushing off the suggestion.

"I understand. I'm a complete stranger. You hardly know me. I guess I can live in my car."

"Live in your car?"

"Well, my landlord is displacing a lot of people. The crunch is on. But it's no big deal. My backseat reclines. No need to worry. I can sleep there, and I can shower at the college."

"I'd let you stay here but most guys can't handle a platonic relationship."

"Yeah, most guys have only sex on their minds," I said as I examined her breasts.

"I'll have to think about it. In the meantime, let's go to work."

I followed her into her dining room where she had a pad and pencil waiting on the table. We sat down.

"I like that idea, Eddie—teaching blind kids to paint."

"Well, if they pay farmers not to grow certain crops, there's got to be a way to fund this concept."

"I like the way you think. Now how do we go about teaching these blind kids to paint?" she asked as she stood up. "Would you like some coffee?"

"Please," I said, then continued. "I learned by numbers. Maybe we can numerically code the colors and shapes, et cetera, and, you know, let them figure it out. There's gotta be a blind Picasso out there somewhere," I said, leaning to watch her move about the kitchen. I marveled at what a lovely ass she had.

"Ah! Excellent!" she said from the kitchen just before she returned to the dining room with two cups of coffee, a sugar bowl and a creamer balanced on a wooden tray.

She sat back comfortably and took the role of an inquisitor.

"Just what is it you're studying, Eddie?"

"Like, what's my major? Liberal arts."

"Why liberal arts?" she asked.

"Because it seems totally useless."

She looked confused for a moment, and then she smiled.

"I never know when you're joking."

"I'm not joking. It's been my observation that the more useless your education and profession are, the less work and more money you make."

"I don't get it."

"Look at any factory. The people doing the real work make

74

nothing. The people playing golf or on extended vacations make all the money."

"So you're only interested in making money?"

"No, I'm really only interested in not working. I had a job once and found it totally unsatisfying."

"What did you do?"

"I sold hot dogs and tacos."

She chuckled and shook her head.

"So, do you have any clue as to what it is you might do with your useless education?"

"Teach. What else do you do with a useless education?"

"I wouldn't go into that if I were you. It's an awful profession."

"Well, you get three months off in the summer, all the holidays, and, hell, you only have to deal with kids."

"Oh, don't get me started! I told you I was a teacher, didn't I? It's not as easy as you think. It's a lot of hard work, and everyone's a critic and thinks he can do it better."

"I have no intentions of doing it better."

She laughed out loud.

"Well, when do you start your student teaching?"

"If I graduate this semester, I'll start in the fall. But, of course, everything's up in the air, now."

"What's the problem?"

"I honestly don't know where I'm going to live," I said, hoping she'd take the hint.

She got a serious expression on her face. She was sizing me up.

"You're really sure about becoming a teacher?"

"How else am I going to avoid work?"

"Well, don't say I didn't warn you." And then she looked at me and laughed. "You've got an odd sense of humor, don't you? Okay, let's get back to business. So we write a proposal teaching blind children to paint..." she interrupted herself, smiled, and even blushed a little. "I think I've made my mind up. Yes, I think it might work out very well."

"What are you talking about?" I asked.

"I've made my mind up! I can hardly wait for you to move in!"

We were gazing into each other's eyes, and I was falling. There was something intriguing about her, and I was captured by it.

Then she interrupted my trance.

"Of course, I expect you to help me with the work around here."

Normally that kind of statement would have set off an alarm. I didn't know what I said or even if I said anything, but I must have accepted this and the one or two other conditions she declared.

I left Ashley's place feeling both exhilarated and confused. I would not live with Alice, yet I was ready to move in with Ashley without even knowing her. In fact, not only had I agreed to do work for her, but I'd acceded without any clear indication that I'd ever get into her pants.

So maybe it was the challenge of seducing her. Or maybe it was because I feared Alice. If Alice would have just given up on the auras and other crap like that, things might have been different.

She was waiting for me on my porch when I returned.

"So, how'd it go with Baba Rama?" I asked.

"He has room for all his children."

"When you moving?"

"Soon enough!" She examined me through an angry squint. "I want to ask you something. Are you seeing that girl?"

"What girl?"

"Don't play coy with me, Eddie Delano!"

Her pretty eyes were ablaze. There was something so appealing about her. If she would only stop talking.

"I know about that girl in your morning class! Everybody on campus knows. The espresso girl at the student union knows, the librarian's assistant knows, and even a stranger—a girl named Barbara McDoogle—told me how much you talk to her. She said you walk her to her car everyday after class!"

"Oh, that one. What about her?"

"Then you *are* seeing her?"

"Um, yeah—as a matter of fact I was just at her place. I was helping her write something."

I was kind of flattered that Alice was so jealous. To be honest, I didn't think she liked me anymore, but maybe I was wrong. Maybe I should work things out with her.

"You're a bastard, Eddie!"

"Relax. There's nothing going on. We're writing proposals to help disadvantaged children. Blind kids, to be specific."

She lit a cigarette and eyed me suspiciously.

"Eddie, there's something you're keeping from me."

76

"Well, she just happens to need a roommate, and I told her about my situation."

Her mouth dropped, and I cringed inwardly. Why did I tell her the truth? That was unlike me.

I tried to rebound.

"Hell, you're going to live at Baba Ramada Inn!"

"You bastard!"

"It's not what you think, Alice. It's platonic. Purely platonic. I need a place to live, desperately, and she needs a roommate."

My emotions ran wild. Her anger revealed a passion I had never seen before. I really didn't know she cared this much. If I had known earlier, maybe things would have been different.

Just then, she had to say it.

"Eddie, your aura is giving me negative vibes."

Of all the goofy things she could say, she had to bring up the auras!

I blurted out at her, "Well, your aura's boring, Alice."

10

Ashley Lychcraft

Graduation became everyone's concern, except mine. I had every intention of avoiding the ceremony, but Winston assured me it was a wise investment.

"The cap and gown will run you a little over twenty-five bucks. Photographs will run another fifteen and announcements another ten. All of it for a grand total of fifty bucks."

"Seriously, Winston. How am I going to turn a profit from this?"

"Well, you've got parents. They'll give you a graduation gift," he said with a wry smile. "Also, there's aunts, uncles, and friends of the family. All of them will more than likely feel obligated to send you something."

"What if they show up for graduation? I'll have to talk to them. They'll probably want to take me out to dinner. Jesus Christ, do you have any idea what a drag that will be?"

"Of course, but there is money to be made doing relatively little work. Besides, I doubt seriously if any of your family would make a trip this far north just to see you. They'll more than likely just send you money."

"Are you going to be there?"

"I don't usually go to ceremonies of my *protégés*, but we Hispanics have to stick together. Can't stay too long, though. I'll be leaving for holiday the day after the grand farce."

I followed Winston's advice, and luck was with me. No one from my family could set time aside from their hectic schedules in order to see me graduate.

The moment the ordeal was over, Winston approached me.

"Not bad," said Winston. "That wasn't too tedious."

"Tedious enough! Let's go grab a beer."

"Not so hasty. Now we have to get a couple of photographs of you and your professors."

Winston shoved me towards Professor Doolittle. He smiled as we approached.

"Gonzales and Delano! My prize pupils."

"Sir, do you think it would be okay if I had my photograph taken with you?" I asked.

"Absolutely, my boy!"

After taking a few snapshots, Winston moved close to me and whispered, "Let's ditch this old windbag and see if we can get a couple more photos of you with a few other profs."

We easily slipped away from Doolittle when he was distracted by several other students.

"Why do I have to get all these pictures taken with my professors, Winston?"

"It will increase the value of your graduation by at least twenty percent. When your parents see the pictures, it will help them with their boasting. It will give them the high ground with their peers."

Imitating a proud father, Winston pretended that he was holding up a photograph for inspection.

"My boy and his professors—et cetera, et cetera."

A week passed, and I had just returned from the post office where I had made a change of address. After I finished packing my books and other valuables into my car, I saw a group of zombies wearing yellow robes at Alice's place. They were chanting gibberish, and they followed her when she approached me.

A feeling of dread knotted my stomach. I sensed that I was making a big mistake.

"Well, Eddie, I guess it's time to say good bye," she said.

I felt a strange pang of sorrow for Alice. Then I realized I had to stop her. She couldn't go off to live with a bunch of oddballs. And what was I doing moving in with Ashley?

"Look, maybe we're both making a big mistake."

There was a glint in her eyes: for a moment, they seemed to come alive. But then her friends shouted for her to join them.

"I don't think so, Eddie. I've made up my mind. I'm giving up on the material world."

"I guess you're right. I'm sorry things didn't work out."

"But they did, Eddie. I've found peace and contentment with Baba Rama."

With that, she kissed me on the cheek. I was about to embrace her when one of the bald chanters pulled her away. Alice took one last glance back at me, and I could see tears in her eyes. I watched as they piled into a van and then drove away from the courtyard.

I returned to my bungalow and retrieved a very large marijuana cigarette that I had found while packing. I was hesitant to smoke anything Sam might have rolled, but it seemed like the perfect occasion to lose myself.

I arrived at Ashley's just as the neurons in my brain cells were short circuiting. I had a difficult time keeping my grasp on reality.

"So this is what it's like to be Sam," I thought aloud.

Then something struck me as I left my car. Maybe it was the joint, but for the first time I realized the poor condition of Ashley's place. The roof on the barn was partially missing, the fences sagged, the gate to the corral was held together by bailing wire, and even the house was slanted at an angle.

Then dread surged through me as I recalled my agreement with her: I was allowed to move in under the condition that I helped her repair her fences and gates and that I would be willing to do other chores around the house. What was I thinking?

Ashley, in a straw hat and overalls, was pruning rose bushes at the side of the house. She walked towards me as I approached.

"You're here just in time," she said. "I need a break. Let me show you around."

Still carrying her shears, she led me around the barnyard, pointing out the different animals.

"I board those horses," she said pointing towards the pasture. "They bring in a little cash. They have to be watered and fed twice a day." She then pointed out by name each of the horses, one at a time, and added, "I really appreciate your offer to help me. It's a lot of work for one person."

Suddenly, a big black dog with floppy ears appeared from behind the barn. My heart stopped. The dog bounded towards me, jumped up and almost knocked me down. He was wagging his tail and trying to lick my face.

"Eddie, meet Zeth," said Ashley. "Oh, he really likes you, Eddie. He doesn't do this to everybody."

I turned my head away from the mutt and pushed him to the ground.

"Zeth just got back from the vet's. I had him neutered," she added.

We walked towards the corral where a single horse stood listlessly watching us.

"That's my new gelding. My mare is away right now. I'm having her bred. She's currently in cohabitation with a magnificent stallion."

We turned back towards the house when we reached the chicken coop.

"I'm keeping the hens for eggs, but as soon as I get a chance, I'm going to have the roosters butchered."

As we approached the house, a huge tabby tomcat jumped out from behind a loose board at the foundation, eyed me suspiciously, and ran under the porch.

"There goes Tom. He stays pretty close to home since I had him cut last spring."

Ashley placed the shears on the wooden rail of the porch, rested her hand on them, and smiled.

"I think you'll like it here, Eddie."

As I unloaded my belongings and carried them through the living room, the odor of cat singed my nostrils. For some reason I did not recall it from my first visit. What I did remember, and I still thought it a little odd, was the large studio photo of Ashley hanging above the sofa. She was cute, but why would she want to look at a picture of herself everyday?

In general, a sense of Ashley dominated the atmosphere of the place. Her degree, teaching certificate and a number of framed awards seemed conspicuously placed throughout various parts of the house. On the mantel there was a collage of pictures from her early childhood through her college graduation. On the wall above the mantel was the Lychcraft family crest: It consisted of something that looked like a gopher holding a pike in front of a shield.

A large bookcase dominated the living room. I glanced at what looked to be a complete collection of Virginia Woolf, Anaïs Nin, Willa Cather and Edith Wharton. Lying on a small table was a copy of *The Bell Jar* by Sylvia Plath.

Aside from the variety of texts every college student accumulated, there seemed to be an absence of books authored by male writers. I saw only one book by Hemingway, *For Whom the Bell Tolls*, and it was squeezed between the works of Gertrude Stein and Dorothy Parker.

Houseplants hung from every window, all of them ill-looking except for her Venus's-flytrap. On a brick-and-board shelf she kept an old stereo system and a stack of well-worn albums by various female singers.

An old faded Persian carpet covered the entire living room floor, and against one of the walls was a large overstuffed chair, a chair that only Ashley was allowed to sit in. It was one of the few spoken rules that she made clear to me from the start. I sat in it anyway.

Several days later Ashley smiled and asked, "Would you give me a hand out back?"

I followed her to a section of fence that had collapsed.

"Damn it!" she said. "I just remembered something. I've gotta go into town for something."

"Well, maybe I can run that errand for you."

"Oh, no. No, it would be a great help if you could fix this fence, though."

"Running errands is my specialty. I assure you it would be no problem at all."

"Are you trying to get out of doing work, Eddie? You knew when you first moved in here that there was a lot of work to do."

"No, no," I lied. "I just figured that I would probably be more useful running errands."

"Well, I can run my own errands, thank you very much. What I need," she said with a flirtatious smile, turning her head ever so slightly, "is help with the fence."

There was no point in arguing with her. She was better at manipulating people than I.

"Okay," I said with a compliant smile. "No problem."

She left, and having absolutely no idea how to fix a fence, I retired to the living room sofa and took a nap. Ashley jolted me from my sleep when she returned several hours later.

"Eddie! You didn't do a thing to the fence!"

"Ah, yeah," I replied as I tried to stand. "I was, um, right in the middle of getting one of those doohickeys that go on the watchamacallits when I realized that I didn't have a thingamajigger."

"Oh," she said apologetically, a puzzled look on her face.

"I'll get it tomorrow. Oh, damn, I forgot. Tomorrow I've got to register for some dumb thing at the college."

"Just when do you think you'll get around to doing the work?"

"Real soon," I lied. "Believe me. I'm really pissed at myself for not fixing the fence. I promise I'll fix it, the first chance I get."

On Tuesday evenings I was supposed to make my presence scarce while Ashley and her women's reading group met for dinner and a discussion.

Three of Ashley's friends drove up in an old Volvo and the other two arrived in old BMW. They all looked pretty much alike in their granny dresses, but one of them was especially unattractive. She had a head of what can best be described as wild blonde pubic hairs.

They all hugged Ashley, and the only time they stopped smiling was when Ashley introduced them to me. The unasked, awkward question was whether or not I was eating dinner with them, which I wasn't—as much to my relief as it was to theirs.

I went to the bookcase and retrieved Virginia Woolf's *Jacob's Room*, a story the group had read several weeks previously. I held it up as I walked back by them.

"Ashley said this was a great book. I'll be out on the back porch reading," I said.

From the back porch I listened to them talking and laughing as they ate and drank. Soon I heard the hissing sound of smokers sucking in the weed, and then the sweet scent of marijuana floated onto the porch. The laughing turned into giggling.

"...and then he actually asked me for my phone number! Can you believe that?" one of them said.

"No," I thought aloud into the open night air.

"And what did you say? I hope you put him in his place!" said a girl with a strident tone of voice. "He's such a macho jerk!"

"I told him I thought he was insensitive," said the first girl.

"What man isn't?" said someone else.

Another one jumped in with, "All they want is wham-bam-thank-you-ma'am! And then they think they own you."

"Men! Who needs them?"

Several voices rose in agreement. Then the strident voice cut through.

"Yeah, Ashley. Why did you get a male roommate?"

My hair stood on end.

"Oh, he needed a place, and I felt sorry for him."

"Has he tried anything?"

"No way! If he does, I'll kick him in the nuts."

They all laughed. Then someone with a little sense spoke up.

"But he *is* kind of cute."

There was an eruption of disapproval. When it died down, Ashley continued.

"Well, he does help out around here. And he did give me that fabulous idea about writing a grant to help blind children to paint."

"Oh, right," said one of them, with a note of approval.

"And he resembles Byron," said Ashley.

"You didn't say that to him, did you?" said the one with the strident voice. "He might get ideas!"

"I'm not sure he knew who Byron was," laughed Ashley. "He said 'Brian who?'"

The others burst out laughing. Eventually the sensible one spoke up again.

"But there *is* something about him. He reminds me of a T.A. named Winston Ashford Gonzales."

"Yes, he does!" one of them squealed in agreement. "But Winston's so tender and gentle."

"And romantic," said the sensible voice.

"You didn't sleep with him, did you?" asked the squealer with a slight note of jealousy.

"No! Did you?"

"No. But I thought about it."

There was a thoughtful silence.

"Whatever happened to him?" asked Ashley.

"He's working on a Ph.D. in philosophy."

"No, it's art history."

"Oh, it doesn't matter."

They all seemed to giggle at once.

"You don't think that Eddie is like Winston, do you?" asked Ashley.

"A little. But Winston would have known who Byron was?"

There was another round of giggles, and then silence.

"Ashley, what is it you want in a man?"

My ears perked up.

"I want someone who's sensitive, who respects my feelings, and gives me my space."

"Who doesn't?" cried out the whole group in unison.

The following morning I sat on the sofa with *Jacob's Room* on my lap, looking out the window as wistfully as I could, without appearing too faggy.

Ashley entered the room, looked at me and asked, "Are you okay, Eddie?"

"Oh, yeah," I said. Then with feigned enthusiasm, "I'm just moved by Woolf's complex..." I paused, as if searching for the right words.

"Stream of consciousness?" she asked, sitting down next to me.

"Yeah, stream of consciousness! Whew!"

"You like it?" she asked with pleasure in her voice.

"Are you kidding? It's amazing!" It was amazing anyone would actually read it.

"I'm surprised. For some reason I just didn't think you would appreciate it. I should have realized..." her voice trailed off. Then she continued with a twinkle in her eye, "Anyone who could conceive of such a wonderful idea to help blind children would certainly be in tune with Virginia Woolf."

A brief moment passed as we gazed into each other's eyes, and then we fell into an embrace. Our clothing left a trail to her bedroom. There we spent the rest of the morning making love.

Later, in an unguarded moment, she stretched her nude body comfortably across the bed and said, "I didn't think it would take you long, Eddie Delano. Now what are you gonna do with me?"

So we did it again.

11

Acquired Deafness Syndrome

At first, sleeping with Ashley was fun. But it wasn't too long after I started sleeping with her that I realized she talked too much.

She wasn't as bad as Alice. At least Ashley occasionally made sense. What made the problem difficult was that she realized I seldom listened to her. But then why should I? She never listened to herself.

She went so far as to quiz me.

"What did I just say?"

"You said something about me never paying attention."

"You don't. And I didn't say anything at all about you not paying attention."

"Okay, what did you say?"

"I said I want you to listen to me!"

When she wasn't badgering me about not paying attention, she was dictating long lists of chores for me to do or soliciting my opinion about the most inane of issues.

And that was how it was—everyday.

Halfway through the summer break, I started to lose my hearing. It happened while I was trying to read the paper one morning. I was reading an article about another act of vandalism claimed by the New People's Army. They had slashed the tires on a custodian's truck. Power to the people, I thought.

Ashley entered the living room, held up two ugly sweaters and asked, "Which do you think looks best—the pink sweater or the beige one?"

"I don't know," I said, returning to the article.

"Come on, Eddie. Put the paper down and pay attention to me. I can't make up my mind."

"Okay, the pink one."

"Oh, no. The pink one is too frilly."

"You're right. The beige one is better. The pink one's too frilly."

"But the pink sweater does go with my complexion, and the beige one is too bulky."

"Yeah, you're right. The beige one is too bulky. The pink one is better. It goes with your complexion."

"But it's too frilly. You said so yourself. I don't understand how you can actually like it more than the beige!"

"You know, you're right. The beige one is too bulky and the pink one is too frilly."

"Make up your mind. I've never known anybody so indecisive."

"Suit yourself, Ashley. Either one is fine with me. I don't have to wear them."

I returned to the paper.

"Give me your undivided attention for just one moment!"

I put the newspaper down and feigned my undivided attention, but she was not appeased.

"I feel like I always have to beg you for your opinion! Please, Eddie, I need the truth."

"The truth? Are you sure you want my opinion?"

"Of course I do. What do you really think?" she asked.

"You promise you won't get angry?"

"Yes! For heaven's sake! Tell me, now!"

"I think you'd be better off with that blue sweater. You know the one."

"What? That's ridiculous! That blue one is the ugliest piece of trash I have! I wouldn't be caught dead in that old rag. I don't know why I still have it around. I should have thrown it away years ago!"

"You asked me for my opinion."

"You have no taste. I should have known better than to ask."

"Then why did you?"

"Because I thought you could help me choose."

"Choose whatever you want." I picked up the paper.

"Don't tell me what to do!"

"Okay, then don't choose what you want."

"Okay I will!"

A few minutes passed and Ashley returned to the entrance of the living room. She was holding two pairs of shoes. I watched her from the corner of my eye. She seemed to be sizing me up at a safe distance. When it seemed appropriate to her to put me through the third degree again, she pleaded like a timid child.

"Eddie, which shoes do you think would go best with the pink sweater? The brown penny loafers or the white running shoes?"

I knew exactly what to do.

"Pardon me?" I said in a louder than normal voice.

"I said," she repeated, "which shoes do you like best?"

"Which shoes are a pest?" I said with a puzzled expression on my face.

"No, I said which shoes are best?"

"Oh, it's a test."

"You're impossible!"

"What's unstoppable?"

"Can't you hear me?"

"Speak up. I can't hear you."

"Oh my God! You're losing your hearing."

"You know, Ashley. I think I'm losing my hearing. It just happened, just this very minute. I felt a strange sensation in my ears the minute you started talking. This is really weird. Say something."

"Can you hear me?"

"I can't hear you."

Soon my deafness became an incredible asset. Ashley stopped asking me to do any work whatsoever. She even stopped talking to me. In fact, she apologized in writing:

> *Dearest Edward,*
>   *I'm so sorry. I've been so selfish. I've*
> *accused you of not paying attention to me*
> *when all along you've been losing your*
> *hearing. Please forgive me.*
>   *Ashley*

Luck was with me for the time being. The only problem now was that Ashley's friends found me interesting. Since I'd first met them, they'd been ignoring me—a blessing I didn't fully appreciate at first. Now they wouldn't stop talking to me.

"You should learn sign language, Eddie!" hollered Martha, the girl with the pubic head of hair.

"Speak more slowly, Martha," I shouted. "Can't hear too well."

"You-should-learn-sign-language-Eddie!"

"Yes it's a fine language," I shouted in reply.

Frustrated, she wrote down her comments and waited for me to respond.

"It's not necessary," I shouted at the top of my lungs. "I'm going to get a hearing aid one day. I'm saving my money."

She wrote down, "There are special grants for students in need of hearing aids."

"Grants?" I shouted.

If only Winston could see me now, I thought.

What must have eventually got to Ashley was that I was sleeping with her, but I didn't have to listen to her. To her mind, it was as if I were getting something for nothing. So she took me to the doctor at the college health office.

The doctor put a set of earphones on my head and turned up the volume.

"Can you hear this?" he asked.

"What?" I said, removing the headset.

"Did-you-hear-anything?" said the doctor.

"No, I can't hear you."

He repeated the question more loudly and I answered no.

"Well," he said to Ashley, "he can't hear too well."

He repositioned the earphones, turned the knob again, and repeated, "Can you hear this?"

I made an inquisitive expression with my eyes and removed the headset again.

"Did you say something? I didn't hear you."

He turned to Ashley and said, "He can't hear anything." Then he looked at me. "However, I don't believe he's entirely deaf."

"Did you say something?" I asked.

"Never mind," said the doctor, with a kind smile.

"Yes, I'm fine." I was getting really good at this.

The doctor addressed Ashley.

"Be patient with him, young lady. He has Acquired Deafness Syndrome."

I knew it couldn't last forever. In fact, being deaf had problems that I hadn't counted on. When I suggested to Ashley one night that we go to the movies, she looked at me with an incredulous expression. I knew right then and there that concerts were also out. In fact, if I wanted to listen to the radio, I had to turn up the volume so loud that I was afraid I really would go deaf.

Faking being deaf was becoming almost as hard as listening to Ashley. Then one morning she confounded my circumstances with a series of probing questions she wrote out on a notepad.

"What are you going to do about your student teaching?"

"I haven't given it much thought," I answered aloud.

"You should think about it." Then she gestured for me to give her a moment longer and wrote, "How will you communicate with your master-teacher, your students, the administrators, the parents, and the theory professor at the college?"

"The same way I'm communicating with you."

A hurt, bewildered expression crossed her face, and she wrote, "How many deaf teachers do you know?"

I was in a bind. I had to buy myself some time to work things out.

"Maybe I can change my major, Ashley."

Her eyes sparkled at the suggestion, and she hastily wrote down, "To what?"

"Remember your grant to teach deaf kids to play the piano? Maybe there's a special scholarship to teach music to deaf veterans."

She smiled, apparently pleased with the both of us, and wrote, "Good idea, Eddie!"

She picked up the pad and left the room. Five minutes later she returned with a long list of chores. At the bottom of the list was written, "When can you help me with these?" and "What color do you think we should paint the bathroom?"

Not only had my lie complicated everything with Ashley, but now she was writing down all the annoying things I didn't want to hear. My deafness had become more of a liability than an asset.

In the meantime, the women's reading group had stopped meeting altogether when it was discovered that Ashley and I were having sex. Martha confessed a lesbian attraction to Ashley, and two of the other women felt betrayed because they had lesbian attractions to Martha. And everybody blamed me.

The only one who did not completely disown Ashley was Sharon.

Sharon. She was a spiteful little creature with beady eyes. She was also recently divorced. Evidently, when her prince charming became her feudal lord and master, she took him to court and lanced him for everything he had.

One day I overheard her complaining to Ashley.

"The men in this town are a bunch of jerks," she said stridently. "They're only good for what you can get out of them!"

"You just haven't found the right one," Ashley said.

I entered the living room and sat across from Ashley and Sharon. Sharon's eyes were ablaze.

"All they want is sex. If I had it my way, we'd castrate all of them. Leave only a few for breeding."

I examined the room for any sharp instruments she might grab hold of.

"Did you say something about bleeding?" I asked.

"Just mind your own business! You don't know what it's like to be a woman!"

Sharon had shouted so loud that I couldn't ignore her, even with my feigned condition.

"Of course not. I'm a man. You're not being fair."

"Women have been fair too long! Now it's our turn to be unfair."

"What did you say about underwear?" I asked with my hand cupped to my ear.

She became an angry caricature of herself. She shook her head in disgust.

I pointed to my ear and said, "Can't hear too well." Then I excused myself and sat at the dining room table pretending to read a magazine and trying not to laugh aloud.

"Ashley," Sharon whispered. "That fool has to go. He's a jerk."

"Why do you say that?"

"Because I think he's a fake. What do you see in him, anyway?"

"He's cute. Besides, he has a poetic quality I like."

"He's the laziest person I've ever seen. He'll never let you grow, you know. Does he do any work at all?"

"Not much. But he has other talents. He's working on a special scholarship so he can return to college and declare a new major in music."

"Give me a break!"

"Come on, Sharon. He has such good ideas."

"I'm not so sure. You know, we were all a little taken in by him when we first met him. He read Virginia Woolf and he helped you with your grant writing. But has he done anything since he started getting what he wanted?"

"Well, not exactly. But it's not his fault. He does try."

"Well, you've got your hands full with *lover boy*, don't you? I just don't see where Eddie fits into the picture."

"Not so loud," said Ashley in a subdued voice.

"Who cares! He's a deaf and dumb jerk. I don't care what he thinks, and neither should you."

I realized I had heard too much. In fact, I couldn't take much more of it. If I listened any longer, they might reveal a lot of other disgusting things that they would never have talked about in my presence, things that I would prefer not to know.

I had to put an end to this fake deafness. I returned to the living room and sat on the floor across from Sharon and Ashley.

"Do you have something for a headache?" I asked.

"What's wrong?" shouted Ashley.

"Not so loud. There's this ringing in my ears," I said.

Sharon's sneer made me realize I couldn't just end the hoax by declaring that I could hear.

"Do you want me to take you to the college health center?" Ashley asked.

"I can manage it myself."

I wandered around the college bookstore, thumbed through some magazines, and then stopped off at the student union for a beer. I was feeling pretty stupid for getting myself caught up in such a dumb lie. Then I heard a familiar voice.

Sitting at the bar in a new Hawaiian shirt, looking tanned and relaxed, was Winston Ashford Gonzales. He was finishing a business transaction with a beautiful redhead.

"Of course not," he said with condescension. "It doesn't matter if the class is closed. For a small donation, I can get you into any class."

The redhead exchanged a twenty dollar bill for what was probably a blank add card with all the necessary permit stamps attached. She was walking away when Winston acknowledged me.

"Delano! Is that you? Come and buy me a beer. You look like shit. What's troubling you?"

I recounted most of the mess I had got myself into, but I purposely left out the part about moving in with Ashley. He would have ridiculed me for that. He had a firm belief that living with women was a disaster that any smart man would avoid.

"Yes, I can see the problems with being deaf. Thank God you had enough sense not to fake being blind. But I do like the idea of returning to school to declare music as a major. There's a real possibility there."

"Yeah, but my whole life is upside down right now."

"I really see no problem at all. Just tell everyone you saw a different doctor. He squirted some kind of experimental cleaning fluid into your ears and now you can hear. Oh yes, you still have headaches and occasionally there's some ringing in your ears, but all and all, you're coming along nicely."

"That's it? Cleaning fluid and a new doctor?" I could not hide my disappointment.

"Look, I didn't get you into this mess. Here I am giving you advice for the price of a beer, and you get testy."

"I'm sorry, Winston. It just doesn't sound believable."

"Eddie, do you know what your problem is? You don't like lying. And the sad thing is, you have such natural talent for it. If I had come up with a gem like being deaf, I could have made a career out of it."

That was the truth. He could have.

We parted company on good terms, but I was haunted by Winston's words. I really did not like lying. I realized that I was a pretty rotten person for deceiving Ashley. Then I started thinking about Alice and how I might have been somehow responsible for her running off to live with Baba Rama.

Guilt was tapping on my shoulder, and I felt I had to set things right, so I bought a six-pack of beer and resolved to tell Ashley the

93

truth. Not the entire truth, but just enough so I wouldn't have to be deaf anymore.

But it wasn't easy, or without consequence. The day after hearing the good news, Ashley put me to work repairing the fence. And that night she approached me with an inquisitive expression.

"Eddie, I know I've asked you this before, but I just want to be certain that I have it right. Which sweater do you think looks best? The beige or the pink one?"

My ears were ringing.

12

Biology and Affordable Housing

There were things I heard while I was deaf that bothered me. For example, I could swear Sharon had said to Ashley something like "you've got your hands full with lover boy" and something about not knowing where I "fit into the picture."

For some as yet inexplicable reason, the words echoed repeatedly in my mind. At first I just assumed I was "lover boy", a name I found utterly disgusting. But why did Sharon say she didn't know where I "fit into the picture"?

And then there were the telephone calls Ashley would take in the closet. Sometimes she would exit the closet exhilarated, and she would ignore me. Other times she would leave frustrated and seek me out for comfort.

I convinced myself I was just being paranoid, but Ashley's dramatic mood swings were making me suspicious. One day she left early in the evening and nearly tore my head off when I asked her where she was going.

"You don't own me! I can go where I want, whenever I want!"

Later that night the creaky floors of the old house betrayed her return. I awoke and heard her footsteps enter the bedroom. I listened to her undress in the dark and then felt the movement of the bed as she slipped between the sheets. She cuddled up to me, and I felt her soft naked body.

"I'm sorry I'm so late. I was with Sharon. She was having a bad day."

I felt her feather-light, shapely body squirm against me, and I detected the faint fragrance of an unfamiliar cologne. It aroused my curiosity, but then she wiggled against me again, and I felt her hand slide down my body. I was no longer preoccupied with my concerns.

About a week passed before a most unpleasant sensation ripped through my penis. I stood before the porcelain bowl and discovered that I had acquired a disease that was said to be brought to this country by indiscriminate sailors.

"Ashley!"

She rushed to my side with a look of concern on her face.

"I think I've got the clap or something!"

"Where could you have gotten that?" she asked timidly.

"From you!" I said with the shock of sudden realization.

"No, you couldn't. It's impossible. No Lychcraft has ever had that. You must've picked it up off a toilet seat."

"You don't get VD from a toilet seat!"

She avoided eye contact.

"Well, maybe you got it from some girl at school."

"I got it from you! Who've you been with?"

"No one," she replied in the timid voice of a guilty child. "Do you really think I would do such a thing?"

"I didn't get this from looking at dirty magazines!"

I was enraged, but I collected myself and decided to take a different approach.

"You know, the health office is going to ask you the same question. Why don't we just save ourselves any future embarrassment?"

She looked away from me, and then in a faint whisper said something I couldn't believe I heard.

"My boyfriend."

"Your *boyfriend*? So that's who *lover boy* is!"

"Don't worry. I told him all about you. He's not jealous."

"Ashley, I thought there was something special between us," I said desperately. "Was I wrong?"

She started to cry.

I began to pack my things.

"What are you doing? Don't go. Please. I'm sorry. I made a mistake."

"No, *I* made the mistake." I wanted to choke her.

"Please, Eddie. We can work it out. I need you," she said in a whimper. "I'll pay all the rent if you stay."

I paused in my packing.

"All the rent?"

For a moment I thought about giving in, but it wasn't really because of her offer, or even her tears. I was really hurt, and I wanted the pain to go away. I wanted things to be the way they were.

But then the fullness of her betrayal worked its way back into my thoughts.

"No! Why don't you have your *boyfriend* move in!"

"He can't. He was picked up last night. He's in jail for violating his parole. He was selling reds to some kids in a junior high school parking lot and they caught him."

"Can you say that again? I swear I thought you said he was selling reds to kids!"

"Oh, don't make me explain. I know he's bad, but he's so beautiful, too."

"He sells drugs to kids, and he's beautiful?"

"You should see him with his hair in the wind, when he's riding his hog."

"He's a *biker* drug dealer?"

She smiled as if I had just asked if he were a brain surgeon.

"Yes. Kevin is just the most gorgeous man I've ever known."

"Wha'da ya see in someone like that?" I blurted in anger.

She tossed her hair back, looked down her nose at me, and said, "He's a *real* man."

The housing crunch was worse than I had anticipated. At the campus housing office, a bored-looking woman addressed me from behind a cluttered desk.

"Things are getting really tight. The word is out about Del Norte. Easy grades and little work. Enrollment is up and housing is down."

"But I'm in a bind. I really need a place to live."

"I'm sorry. There hasn't been a single new listing all week."

She pointed to the board where only two rental cards were left. As I approached them, she read one aloud from memory.

"Born-again Mary. Mandatory church attendance."

"Sounds awful. The other can't be that bad."

"Not if you're gay."

I read the other card aloud, "Desperate homosexual. Promises to be gentle."

I looked back at the woman gloomily.

She shrugged. "What can I say? Come back in the afternoon. Something might come in."

I returned several hours later and found the housing office empty. There was only one card left on the corkboard—Born-again Mary.

As I stood there, the thought of living with Born-again Mary reluctantly crossed my mind. I could live out my period of student teaching incognito. So what if I had to go to church once in a while. I did it in the army to get out of KP and guard duty. Hell, the first sergeant thought I was the most pious soldier he had ever seen.

Suddenly, there was someone behind me.

"Hallelujah!" he yelled. "A Christian woman! Praise the Lord, I've found a home!"

He was a young man wearing a white shirt and a black tie, and he was carrying a Bible.

"Not so fast. I saw it first," I said, grabbing the index card from the board.

"But you have no idea how hard I've looked for a decent place to live. I've had to live with Buddhists, pot-smoking astrologers, communists, fornicators, and even a bisexual vegetarian. It's been awful! Please, look into your Christian heart and find the mercy and generosity our Lord has taught us to have."

"Tough luck," I said. "I've had it pretty bad myself."

"Give me that number," he said firmly. His fist was clenched.

"Hell no."

"In the name of God, give me that number!"

"What kind of a Christian are you, anyway?" I asked, hoping to play upon his religious faith. The last thing I remember was a fairly large fist approaching my face.

When I came to, he was gone, and so was the index card that had Born-again Mary's phone number. Dejectedly, I shoved my hands into my pockets, took a deep breath, and walked away.

Eventually, I found myself walking towards the student union. Then Winston Ashford Gonzales appeared before me out of nowhere, like Mephistopheles himself.

"Say it again. This time with a little less English."

He was tutoring a young Hispanic student. The young man was wearing baggy beige trousers and a tweed jacket with leather patches. He held a pipe in his hand.

Winston spotted me and called out, "Delano! Come quick." He turned to his pupil. "This, Hector, is the one-and-only Edward Delano." Then he turned back to me. "My God, Delano! What's happened to your eye?"

"What are you talking about?"

"Your eye! It's black and blue. And swollen."

"I ran into a Christian."

"That figures," he said curtly. "Edward, I don't mean to change the subject, but can you say 'hardly' and show this cretin how it's done?"

"*Hardly.*"

"There! Hector, can you hear how a pro does it? And Delano was once just like you." He looked at me. "Hector sounds either like Charles Bronson or Peter Pan. He just can't seem to get it right."

Returning his attention to his pupil, Winston Ashford Gonzales announced, "Hector, you're dismissed for the day. Be here tomorrow promptly at noon, and practice saying 'hardly', 'of course' and 'come now'." Then he turned to me. "Delano, let's grab a beer at the pub. Your treat, of course."

We watched Hector lope away, mumbling "of course" and "come now" in rhythm to his stride.

"The poor fool is hopeless," said Winston as we turned towards the student union. "He has everything in the world going for him. He's a veteran, his family's income is below the poverty level, and he is, of course, Hispanic. Yet, he's only recently applied for grants. He actually had a job when I found him! You know, I'm fed up with these charity cases. If he can't say 'hardly' correctly by tomorrow, he's on his own."

Then he sensed I was troubled and asked, "What's eating you, Edward. Caught cheating on an exam? Is it the South Sea Islander thing?"

"Nothing, Winston."

"Please, don't try to fool me. You've got a cloud over your head. Is it a woman?"

I must have flinched.

"Bingo!" He smiled. "Who is she?"

"Her name is Ashley"

"Lychcraft? No! You've got yourself in a jam, all right. The woman's mad. Her family does have a lot of money, though."

99

"You know her?"

"Of course. She used to be called 'Our Lady of Del Norte' by my Catholic colleagues. You're not in love with her, are you?"

"I don't know. I feel awful when I'm around her."

He said nothing, waiting.

"It's weird, Winston. Sometimes I can't stand her. She talks non-stop and makes little sense."

"Yes, yes," he muttered as if I were stating the obvious.

"But when I think about not being with her, I kind of miss her."

"This is serious, Edward. How could you fall into such a state? Have you considered therapy?" Then he stopped and looked at me suspiciously. "You haven't been living with her, have you?"

I didn't answer him.

"Delano, I'm disappointed in you!"

"I needed a place to live! I was desperate. And she's got such a fine ass."

He said nothing for a moment or two.

"Well, considering it's you, I suppose that's not such a bad reason to live with her. Yes, I can see the possibilities. Does she cook?"

"Sometimes. But not very well."

"Does she clean and take care of you?"

"Not really."

"But she does have a fine ass. I know this to be true. And her family does have a lot of money. So what's the problem?"

"She gave me the clap."

"Oh, how rude!"

"You know, I didn't think I'd feel this way about her. At first, I figured I could sort of live with her until something better came along. But when she told me about the other guy..." I paused, considering. "I don't know. I felt different about her."

"I suppose she asked you to leave."

"No, she begged me to forgive her. She even offered to pay all of the rent."

"Well, there you go. What can be so bad about that? Can't you find it in your heart to forgive the little tart?"

"Not after what she's done! She gave me the clap!"

"A man of principles. You've really got to get a handle on this, Edward. If you ask me, I'd forgive her. After all, no rent and a fine ass are a wonderful combination."

100

I did as Winston suggested, but I didn't like the way it was working out. Ashley was conciliatory at first, but when we went to the student health office the next morning, she promptly informed the staff that I had given her VD.

The doctor gave me a shot and a dirty look.

"You'd better keep your pecker zipped up, stud!"

After the visit we avoided each other. A chilly week and a half passed like a kidney stone before Ashley finally broke the silence.

"You know, if you took care of my nesting instincts and did more around this place to make it feel like a home, I wouldn't have had a need for the affection I got from Kevin."

"You mean it's my fault?"

"Well, yes. But I forgive you."

"How big of you," I said bitterly. "You give me a venereal disease, and you forgive *me*?"

This gave her pause, but she recovered brilliantly. A wistful look crossed her face.

"Well, it's also your fault because you never..." she stopped herself. "Never mind."

"Never mind what?"

She looked at me with resolve.

"Well, you never told me you loved me."

"*That's* why you screwed Kevin?"

"Yes," she said simply. "It was your fault."

I was speechless. I went to the porch, sat on a bench and looked out over the garden that was withering away because of neglect. In the distance I could see the crest of Sugar Loaf Ridge highlighted in the late afternoon sun. It should have been a pleasant view, but I was preoccupied.

Soon the barn and chicken coop were casting grim shadows across the yard, and the horses were meandering towards the fence, anticipating their evening feeding.

Ashley crept up behind me and wrapped her arms around me.

"I gotcha," she said.

If I had any sense at all, I would have pushed her away. But I felt her loose, supple breasts rub against my back and I became confused.

101

Despite my better judgment, I was stirred by her.

And then I realized something. We were all victims of chemicals splashing around inside us. They betrayed us. They made us do things we knew were not good. But we were helpless to our hormones. We were trapped.

God had cursed us with our own biology. And with housing shortages.

She kissed me, and the blood from my brain rushed to my dick.

13

One Dead Horse

I wasn't sure if I would stay with Ashley or not. But when the first of the month came and she was good for her word, I figured I could be big enough to overlook her indiscretion. After all, paying no rent had advantages that couldn't be overlooked.

Now, the only problem was her nagging. I was scolded for one thing or another on an hourly basis.

"Eddie, did you pick up after yourself?" And, "Eddie, did you make the bed?" And, "Did you take out the garbage?" And, "How many times do I have to tell you to eat with your mouth closed!" And, worst of all, "Put the toilet seat down!"

On this last issue, I stood my ground.

"You never pick it up after you're done with it. Why should I put it down when I'm finished?" But my logic was beyond her grasp, and it was met with open hostility.

What made the situation worse was that her poor ability to compromise went beyond our relationship. A case in point was the drama that brewed between herself and Suzy, a twelve-year-old girl whose sick horse became the center of our lives for the next three weeks.

"I knew that little bitch would do it! I've told her a thousand times not to race her horse back into the pasture. She never cools him down, and she feeds him cheap oat hay. I warned her that if Pops got sick, I was going to kick him out. So out he goes!"

"Isn't that a little harsh?"

"He'll endanger the others." She lit a cigarette. "You said you wanted to learn about horses. Here's your chance to do something useful for a change. Go get Pops and tie him up to the telephone pole on the street. I'm calling Suzy and telling her to come get her horse."

"Can't you put him in a separate stall?"

She responded with a cold, silent stare. I continued.

"If you don't want the horse, nobody else will either, especially on this short notice."

"That's Suzy's problem!"

"Why don't you give the kid a break. It's going to be hard enough on her when she learns that her horse is sick."

"It will teach her a lesson."

"The only thing she's going to learn is that you're heartless."

"Okay, fine. You take care of the horse! You isolate him! You give him his medication!"

"Wait a second. Let's not be hasty here. What do I know about horses?"

"You'll learn."

A veterinarian was called, and he administered penicillin to Pops. Ashley announced that I was to administer the remainder of the dosage. When it was time, I reluctantly approached the horse. Mucus ran from his nose, and worse—there was a loud rattle in his breathing.

Ashley stood nearby with her hand on her hip and her head cocked to the side. The smirk she wore was the final brushstroke to the portrait of impatience.

"Are you sure you want me to do this, Ashley?" I asked, hoping she would have a change of heart.

"You really disappoint me, Eddie."

Disappointing Ashley was not going to improve her disposition.

"Okay, here goes," I said.

She smiled, showing her approval. I stood there in silence, hopelessly trying to remember how the vet had done it.

"Look," she said impatiently. "First you wrap the chain around Pops' nose and tighten it, just like the vet did."

"Isn't that going to hurt him?"

"Yes!" she said impatiently. "It should hurt him very much!"

"Let me rephrase my question. Isn't that going to anger him?"

"Maybe, but it will keep his mind off of this," she said, producing a long needle attached to a syringe. "And do it just like the vet did. Jab him, then draw it upwards. If blood comes up, then you inject the needle someplace else."

"Is that necessary? I mean, why can't I just inject it anywhere?"

"Didn't you listen to the man when he was here?"

"No. I was nauseated."

"Well, listen now! If you see blood in the syringe, it means that you hit a vein. If you inject the penicillin into the bloodstream, the horse might die."

"You have a handle on the situation. Why don't you do it?"

"Why should I do it when I can get you to do it for me? Besides, you've got to overcome your fear of horses."

"You're certain they're vegetarians?"

I was answered with another smirk, so I complied with her wishes.

Pops recovered in a short time. By the end of the first week, it was clear he would not die. The following week he seemed healthy enough to leave the stall. But something was not right. Upon his release into the corral, one of the other horses threw a kick, squarely hitting Pops on his side.

"Ashley, why do you suppose that black horse kicked Pops?"

"Horses do strange things."

Then all of the horses in close proximity to Pops either bit him or kicked him.

"You can tell they take care of their own," I said.

"Make sure he gets his share when you feed them," she said.

"How am I supposed to do that?" I asked.

She answered my question by reminding me that the garden needed tending. "And don't forget that section of fence I told you about," she added as she walked away.

It was the middle of the night, and I found myself wide awake and wondering how I'd got myself into this ridiculous situation. Reasoning would always return me to the fact that I didn't pay any rent.

I got out of bed and went to the window. The fog was low and the horses were stirring. Suddenly there was a crashing sound. I went to investigate.

In the gray mist that reflected the light from my flashlight, I saw the outline of a horse's legs thrashing back and forth in the air. It was Pops. He was on his back in a bathtub used as a trough.

Horses do strange things, I thought.

I scoured the yard in search of a long two-by-four to use as a lever. When I found one, I placed it under Pops' body and applied pressure. He violently thrashed to-and-fro as he desperately struggled to free himself.

Then Ashley came outside and, together, we turned the bathtub over. Pops fell out and staggered to his feet. His back legs collapsed under him. His front legs held firm, but as much as he struggled, he could not use his back legs. He quivered. It was clear that it was only a matter of time before he would die.

Ashley made the call, and soon after, Suzy and her mother arrived. Ashley greeted them with the grim news. I could see their breath turn to vapor as it hit the early morning air. Suzy sobbed at the news.

At Ashley's request, our neighbor, Mary Ann, came to our assistance. Mary Ann was a large, muscular old woman who had come to California from Oklahoma during the dust bowl era.

She handed me her twelve-gauge shotgun and spoke in a voice that could only have been produced by a large dose of testosterone.

"Here, take this an' do what ya gotta do."

Suzy's mother nodded a reluctant approval. Then she and her daughter went with Ashley and Mary Ann to the house.

"What do you want me to do with this, Ashley?" I called after them.

"You know what has to be done," Ashley said from the porch and then followed the others inside.

I stood alone in the corral looking at this poor dumb horse.

"I knew it was a waste of time giving you that penicillin," I said.

The horse made some kind of guttural sound. Then the other horses, who had been sadistically playing in the pasture, moved to the fence and watched quietly for a few moments. One of them whinnied. It was an "Adios, pardner. See you in that big pasture in the sky." Then they turned towards the open pasture and fled at a full gallop, neighing like strange creatures in the morning fog.

"Don't take this personally," I said to Pops. "It's just as hard on me as it is on you."

Then Ashley came back out onto the porch and yelled, "You going to talk that horse to death or shoot him?"

"Why don't you come over here and show me how it's done?" I yelled back.

The door slammed in reply.

Then all of the animals broke their silence. The goat, pigs and chickens became agitated. Even the cat looked restless.

I pointed the barrel of the shotgun at Pops' head as he struggled to stand. It would have been easier if he had just fallen down and died, but he was hanging on. With the shotgun snugly held against my shoulder, I recalled the moment I shot off my toe to get out of the army. Using a gun to solve a problem was becoming too easy.

I closed my eyes and pulled the trigger. I was aware only of the walloping kick and the sound, and I imagined the spray of something I didn't want to see.

I opened my eyes and saw Pops still standing. I had missed. But he was scared shitless now and trying to escape from me. It was either more than his body could bear or he was simply obliging me, but at that moment, he dropped dead.

Moments later, Mary Ann, Suzy and her mother left. I felt cold sweat run down my forehead and went behind the stall to vomit.

The following morning was no different than any other summer morning, with the exception of the dead horse in the corral. I avoided Ashley for as long as I could, but eventually she cornered me. She wanted me to feed the animals, do some gardening, and fix another section of the fence.

On Mary Ann's recommendation, Ashley called someone to haul away the carcass of the former Pops. According to Mary Ann, the guy was kind of dumb and slow, but cheap.

He arrived in the early afternoon driving an old Chevy pickup truck with a hoist above the bed. My jaw dropped when I recognized the driver.

It was Sam.

His hair was much longer and he was wearing Indian beads, feathers, and moccasins laced up to his knees. He greeted me like a long-lost friend.

"Eddie, do you know this person?" whispered Ashley.

Sam grinned and nodded his head in approval as I introduced him and explained our past association to Ashley.

Good-naturedly, Sam added, "You know, Ashley. You seem real familiar. I've met you someplace before, haven't I?"

"I don't think so, Sam. I'd remember," said Ashley.

"By the way, Sam. A subhuman creature named Hog came by shortly after you left."

Ashley's eyes expanded, and a look of recognition briefly crossed her face.

"No problem, Eddie," Sam said. "I took care of that a long time ago. No more speculating in psychedelic commodities. I got me a new business hauling stuff and rototilling gardens." Then, wearing that marijuana-induced moronic smile, he added, "Say, Eddie. Whatever happened to Alice?"

A suspicious glance was cast my way by Ashley, who seized the opportunity.

"Who's Alice, Eddie?" she asked with a smirk.

"Just an old friend," I replied.

Sensing that something was going wrong, Sam quickly changed the subject.

"Where's the horse?"

"Follow me," I said.

We opened the old wooden gate and walked into the corral. Flies had made a home on the body.

"Wha'da ya do with dead horses?" I asked.

"I take 'em to the glue factory."

He backed his truck into the corral. As he attached a chain around the ankles of the dead animal's front legs, a family of three in a station wagon drove into the driveway. Evidently, they were responding to the sign Ashley had placed near the road which read, "Horses boarded: Tender loving care."

The father was in his mid-forties. The mother looked a little younger. Their daughter was about Suzy's age. They were the portrait of the average American family. Too polite to comment on the dead horse lying in the corral, they smiled as Ashley greeted them and quickly directed them away from the sight of the carcass.

Sam pulled a lever and the dead horse was dragged across the barren patch of earth and lifted up off the ground. The hoist groaned and bowed slightly, but held firm.

Ashley and the polite family walked back by us to their car. I heard Ashley telling them, "And the pasture is safe and clean."

As we started to lower the dead horse, which was now suspended in midair above the bed of the truck, I heard the father say, "We'll bring our horse over tomorrow."

At that moment, Sam moved a lever and, unceremoniously, the carcass dropped heavily into the bed of the truck.

The family drove away, and Ashley announced that she was walking over to Mary Ann's. I went to the house and returned with a couple of beers.

"Well, Eddie, I finally found myself. Got me my very own business."

"Yes, it looks good," I lied.

"Got me a cabin up behind Sugar Loaf, too. It's far out, dude. I've been poaching salmon, and growing pot, and picking psychedelic shrooms. I even had a far-out party with a bunch of naked girls."

"That sounds interesting." I was not lying. "Where exactly is this place?"

"I'll draw you a map." And he did, complete with a pirate's X to mark the spot where he lived. "Come up anytime. We can go swimming and smoke some outrageous pot. You know, I still owe you one. If you need anything, Eddie, just look me up."

I thanked him, folded the map and put it in my pocket. We finished our beers, reminiscing about the good old days.

"You know, Eddie. It's none of my business, but you don't seem too happy. Do you ever see Alice?"

"No. But I think about her. I wasn't entirely fair with her."

"I hate to say it, but I think Alice would have..." he stopped himself. "I have no business interfering."

Then, assuming a businesslike attitude, Sam opened the door of his cab and picked up a receipt book lying on the seat.

"Well, let's see now." He scratched his head. "That should be 'bout ten dollars."

I exchanged money for the receipt. As he drove away I read it.

"One dead horse—ten dollars."

14

Herbert Spencer Junior High

The simple life on the farm came to an end when the fall semester began. I was about to begin my student teaching. The education department arranged for me to teach eighth graders at a local junior high school.

Shortly before starting my program, I went on campus to purchase my texts for the theory course that accompanied student teaching. I was sitting at a table in the Student Union Building drinking coffee and thumbing through one of the texts, *Why Johnny Can't Teach*, when Winston Ashford Gonzales pulled up a chair and sat across from me.

"Tell me it ain't so, Edward!" He seemed very upset with me.

"What ain't so?"

"Tell me that we didn't come this far in your career to squander it all in a public school." He shook his head, emphasizing his disgust. "The word is out that you're working on a teaching credential."

"I thought you knew this was my plan all along."

"I just assumed it was a passing fancy. Do you have any idea what you're getting yourself into?"

"Certainly. Three months off every summer, two weeks off at Christmas, one week at Easter. Have I left anything out?"

"I thought your goal was to avoid working?"

"How much work can there possibly be? I mean, I'll only be dealing with children."

"Sometimes, Delano, you really surprise me." He paused for a moment. "I suppose next you'll tell me that you plan on getting married. Honestly, did I overestimate you?"

"Winston, please. Give me some credit. I pay no rent living with Ashley, and I'm certain that this teaching business will turn out to be profitable."

"You'll find out soon enough, I suspect. Don't say I didn't warn you."

I was about to register my resentment to his meddling when, at that moment, a loud explosion interrupted us. We rushed outside. A Dumpster behind the quad was ablaze.

Then someone on a bullhorn shouted.

"Down with oppression! Long live the New People's Army!"

"What do these people have against Dumpsters?" I asked Winston.

"I have no idea. Last week they destroyed a broom closet in the east wing of the library." He shrugged his shoulders. "Well, I'd better be off now. Take care of yourself, Edward," he added curtly.

I arrived at Herbert Spencer Junior High at what seemed to me the ungodly hour of 7:35 a.m. Only then did I realize, to my dismay, that this was the time I'd be expected to be here everyday!

Still a little groggy, I examined the classroom. The working conditions were wretched. A large poster of Huckleberry Finn with a caption that read "Reading Is Fun" flapped in the breeze that flowed in through a broken windowpane. Beneath the poster, the original bright yellow paint shone in contrast to the faded yellow on the rest of the walls.

My master-teacher wandered into the classroom, apparently preoccupied. She was a thin, wizened-faced woman, whose thick red lipstick smeared like grease the butt end of her cigarette. Then she noticed me, took one last drag from her cigarette, and put it out in the trash can.

"I'm Jackie Van Dingle," she said shaking my hand. "You must be Edwin Delano."

"That's Edward Delano," I said, correcting her.

"Okay, Edwin, I realize that today's college graduates are illiterate, so let's get one thing straight. You're going to have to get past me if you want your teaching credential. You understand, buster?"

"Yes, ma'am," I replied.

She squinted and studied me from behind purple horn-rimmed glasses.

"Let's see if you're *really* ready to teach. I want you to take this test I wrote."

Mrs. Van Dingle handed me an eighth-grade grammar test and pointed to one of the desks.

"I'm the last of a dying breed, Mr. Delano," she said. "I got my degree in general education. Then I went on for a master of arts degree in education. You see, I'm not like one of these single-subject people who may thoroughly know their subject, but only have a smattering of educational theory behind them. I'm all theory, and I put it into practice."

When I finished, I approached her with the test papers.

"I'm confused about number seven, Mrs. Van Dingle. It asks, 'Which of the following is correct: A) Between you and I; B) Between I and you; C) Among we children; or D) Both C and A.'"

"Is it too hard? I really can't lower my standards."

"No, it's not too hard. It's that none of them are correct."

"Let me see that. Well, it's letter A, for heaven's sake."

"But that's wrong."

"I've been using this test for fifteen years, young man, and in that time my students have done good enough with it!"

"Maybe they changed the rules since I was a kid," I said.

"There have been many major advances in educational theory since you were a student," she said.

She picked up my test papers and went through them quickly, with a practiced eye.

"Hmm, you did very good on every answer but number seven, which you left blank. I'm surprised you did so well. Us teachers at Herbert Spencer have long held the belief that Del Norte was an inferior college."

I said nothing. She lowered her glasses in order to peer over them at me.

"You seem sincere enough, Mr. Delano. But before we begin, I want to show you my methodology." She smiled proudly and proclaimed, "I use flow charts."

She pulled on an old movie screen attached to the wall above the blackboard, drawing it from its container. She let go and the screen snapped back. She pulled it down again, and again it snapped back. She found a hammer and nail in her desk and said to me, "Edwin, hold this for me, please."

As I held it down, she nailed the screen to a well-worn spot on the wall just below the chalkboard. She then turned on an overhead projector and projected onto the screen the reflection of a clear transparency, which she then used to write on with a black grease marker.

"Why don't you use the blackboard?" I asked.

"Today's teacher must learn to utilize modern technology."

She quickly mapped out a flow chart on the transparency.

"You see, Edwin, a student starts here and follows these steps," she explained, pointing to a location on her flow chart. "If he doesn't understand what he's doing at this point," she moved her hand, "then he can go to this point."

I had no idea what she was talking about.

Suddenly, a nerve-shattering buzzer sounded.

"That's the warning bell," she said nervously.

"Are we under attack?"

"No, it means the students have seven minutes to get to class. They'll be here in about ten minutes. Mr. Delano, I want you to observe the last of a dying breed. A real professional educator."

Just then, the vice principal stepped in. He stood about 5 feet 4 inches in his elevated shoes, and he wore a purple bow tie with blue speckles. He was one of those balding men who parted his remaining hair over from the side of his head in a vain effort to cover his shiny scalp. A pair of black horn-rimmed glasses fit crookedly over the bridge of his nose.

"I'm Vice Principal Van Dingle. You must be Mr. Delampre, the new student teacher," he said, grinning, as he vigorously shook my hand.

I didn't bother to correct him on my name.

"I'm a great admirer of Mrs. Van Dingle's work," he said, "even if she is my sister-in-law. You should thank your lucky stars you have her as a mentor. She's got great teaching techniques. Those flow charts of hers are extraordinary."

Another loud buzzer jarred my senses. The man became clearly agitated.

"Good luck, Delampre. I must be out of here before the kids arrive. I like to have as little to do with them as possible."

A moment after he left, a flood of loud, obnoxious apple-cheeked youngsters pushed their way through the door, calling each other "motherfucker" and "faggot." Once seated, they continued

113

their name calling and began shooting rubber bands at each other. One boy walked across the room, punched another boy in the face, and then returned to his desk.

Oblivious to their behavior, Mrs. Van Dingle took roll. Then she returned several homework assignments and distributed dittoed copies of the flow charts that she was about to present on the screen in front of the room.

Her students behaved as if she were a total stranger, someone who had as much authority in their lives as a busboy in a busy restaurant. One student dropped his pencil, and it landed several feet from Mrs. Van Dingle.

The little blond boy, all of thirteen years old, spoke loudly and commandingly.

"Hey, get my pencil!"

Mrs. Van Dingle, like a trained chimp, happily picked it up and smiled as she returned it to him.

"Here you are, Jimmy."

Jimmy returned to his conversation, and I overheard him complaining about his math teacher, Mr. Leonard.

"That fag tried to give me homework. So I told him if he gave me less than a B, I'd report him for child abuse."

Van Dingle proceeded to give her instruction using numerous flow charts. She went from one transparency to another, pointing to a behavior chart, then a work-studies chart, then an extra-credit chart, then a friendship chart, and then a good-citizenship chart. All of these seemed to have some sense of logic, but the detail of her elaborate structure left out one essential ingredient: her lessons.

I thought I had seen enough, but she repeated this routine the following hour. By the time her next class had followed her through her maze of organization, class was nearly over. Van Dingle announced as much and, at that point, all of her students left their desks, shoving each other and calling each other names just as they had when they had entered the class. As they lined up before the door, their anxiety level reached a fevered pitch.

Then the obnoxious bell rang, and the entire class, like a shot gun blast of tiny pellets, exploded out the door and flew in the direction of the snack bar.

Triumphantly, her hands on her hips, Van Dingle exclaimed, "You see, Mr. Delano. That's how a real pro handles a class."

114

She turned off the overhead projector, looked back at me, and said, "We're on break, Edwin. Now run along to the faculty lounge and meet some of the other teachers."

As I entered the lounge, I took a deep breath, and my lungs rebelled against the acrid fumes of tobacco. I coughed.

I noticed an odd-looking man in his late fifties sitting alone near the door and cradling a brown paper bag in his arms. He had sensitive facial lines that suggested the appearance of someone who may have once been scholarly, but had long ago gone completely mad.

Suddenly, he shouted.

"Sit down! Ignoramus!"

At first I thought he was shouting at me, but then I realized he was addressing the wall opposite him. He was now partially bent over, hugging the paper bag as if it might jump off his lap and run away. And he was drooling.

I scanned the dreary room. It was furnished with dilapidated sofas and caste-off tables and chairs. At a weathered cafeteria table, two aging women sat listlessly smoking cigarettes and talking to each other about their diets.

"If I eat any meat, I'll pay for it. Bloat up like a pig."

"Yep, I always eat lots of fruit. Fruit in the morning, fruit in afternoon, fruit in the evening."

"Gotta keep regular. That's what I always say."

"Yep, fruit in the morning, fruit in the afternoon, fruit in the evening."

"Keeps you regular."

"Yep."

The crazy man who was affixed to his brown paper bag again shouted.

"Sit down, you fool! Ignoramus!" And then he resumed drooling, and he rocked himself back and forth on his chair.

My attention was drawn to the door as an awkward, overweight woman entered and eagerly greeted me.

"Mr. Delano, I'm Mimi Van Dingle! I teach health. I hear you're not married."

I flinched, but maintained my composure. "Van Dingle. That seems to be a common name around here."

"Just what do you mean by that?" she said, her Porky Pig face turning into a scowl.

115

"I mean, I never heard the name before coming to this school."

"I can't help it if I'm a Van Dingle! Believe me, it's a cross to bear!"

"I'm sorr—"

"You don't have to say anything. It's written all across your face." She placed her hands on her hips, her torso shaking involuntarily, and shouted, "Nepotism! Right? People think just because I'm a Van Dingle, a teaching job comes easy. Just because my uncle is a vice principal and my father is the assistant superintendent and my mother is the superintendent's secretary, everyone thinks it's easy!"

"I didn't mean anything by it," I said as she walked away. My head was spinning.

I seated myself next to a stout middle-aged, balding man. He wore a cheap-looking blue polyester suit. His face was wide and masked by large pores that looked as though they had been scoured clean with a bristled brush.

"Who are you?" he asked with the severity of a drill sergeant.

"I'm a student teacher."

"So, you want to ruin your life. You want to be a teacher. What a noble thing to do!"

"You sound bitter."

"Bitter? Me, bitter? Naw, I'm not bitter! I'm just pissed off! Look around this place. See that miserable excuse of a human being?" He was pointing to the mental case, who was now staring at his brown paper bag. "He used to be young and idealistic, just like you. You know what happened to him?"

"No," I said timidly.

"*Teaching* happened to him. Go be a truck driver, collect garbage, or sell dope. Find something that people respect!"

The drooling teacher interrupted us as he stood up and again shouted at the wall.

"Wise up, punk! You lazy fool!"

I thought I had seen the worst of it, but Mrs. Van Dingle's sixth period class made her other students look like Rhodes scholars. These children must have been the first in the long evolution of their families to walk upright.

116

Before class started, there was a girl fight. Some things never changed. Girl fights were always worse than boy fights. Boys fought for domination; girls fought until one was either maimed for life or mortally wounded.

Vice Principal Van Dingle was called in and, as he assisted in the break up of the ruckus, another dispute was growing between two brothers who wanted the same seat. Only the momentary realization that blood had been spilled by one of the two girls distracted them long enough for the boys to forget their territorial dispute. I learned later that both of them suffered from severe memory loss, so their bickering rarely lasted long. Both would forget what they were arguing about and do something else until the next conflict would arise.

I could see why so many teachers favored legalized abortions. Even the veteran Mrs. Van Dingle, who had managed to repeat her flowchart lesson five times throughout the day with no more distress than a yawn, was visibly strained at day's end.

When I got home that day, I sat listlessly on the sofa and wondered what had happened to me. Ashley sat across from me.

"What's wrong, Eddie? You seem so exhausted."

"I think I'm going to quit. I've made a mistake."

"But it's only your first day."

"It isn't what I thought it would be."

"But you haven't even started yet."

"Do you know that I'm not going to have enough books or desks for all of my students? And my sixth period class? Forget it! It's filled with kids who are only marginally human."

"Oh, no. You're starting to sound just like a teacher already. Complain, complain, complain. But it can't be too difficult," she said, reminding me of my own words. And then, with a wicked smile, "I told you so."

That night the anxiety of teaching kept me awake. Ashley seemed almost as restless. She tossed and turned, squirming incessantly, but she did not wake. As I sat up, resigned to my insomnia, I thought I heard her moan someone's name.

Then she said something I could swear sounded like, "Ram me, Big Bull Daddy."

Adrenalin flooded my body, and I lay down wide awake until I convinced myself it had been only my imagination.

Then I laughed, thinking how ridiculous it would be for someone as delicate and feminine as Ashley to say such a thing.

15

Theory and Practice

On Tuesday nights the current crop of student teachers met on the sixth floor of Tusk Tower, where the education department was located. Our educational supervisor, Dr. Firman Van Dingle, Vice Principal Van Dingle's brother, conducted the seminar in which we were to discuss the blending of educational theories with practical experience.

Almost six feet tall, Dr. Van Dingle stood in direct contrast to his shorter brother at Herbert Spencer Junior High. He gave the impression of a man who had lived an easy life. Aside from his doughy white skin, he was perfect in his appearance, not a hair out of place. His shirt was starched and his expensive shoes held a rich shine.

"I loved teaching," Dr. Van Dingle began. "I loved it so much that I left it to do educational research. In fact, I have authored all three of your educational texts, two of which, I'm afraid, we will not be able to use this semester."

I didn't like Dr. Van Dingle, but it wasn't because he was a phony. Indeed, I admired the way he could keep a straight face when he spoke. What I didn't like was that he cost me money.

"Dr. Van Dingle," I said. "If we're not going to use two of the texts, why are they required for the course, and why did we have to buy them?"

"Well, that's a good question. You see, as the author of the books, I receive royalties. And I could hardly survive on the meager wages the university pays its instructors."

"But that's unfair," I said without thinking.

"Young man, I have a bad feeling about your future. The ranks of the teaching profession are already overrun with malcontents, what with their unions and demands for such things as due process.

119

You'd better watch your step, or you may find yourself losing your candidacy."

"Dr. Van Dingle, I'm Mary Fitzsimmens," said a mousy-looking student teacher waving her hand. "I think you're right. My father is a principal and he says the big problem today in education is that teachers expect too much respect for what they do."

"Your father couldn't be more correct. And that leads us to the one remaining text that we will be using, *Knowing Your Place: A Guide for New Teachers*. Please open your books to the table of contents. As you can see for yourselves, this is a comprehensive text. It takes you from those first uncertain days of student teaching through those golden years as an administrator. Your first chapter is titled 'The Teacher Is Always Wrong'."

"When do we get to 'Chapter 30, Looking Out for Number One'?"

"It's you again. What is your name?"

"Delano, sir. Edward Delano."

"Delano. It figures. One of those foreign-sounding names. Mr. Delano, Chapter 30 is for administrators—particularly principals. Since it's more than likely you won't be with us much longer, I'd completely ignore it if I were you."

"Good for you, Dr. Van Dingle!" said Mary Fitzsimmens. "You handled Delano like a real pro!"

"Why, thank you, Mary. You know, I have a good nose for spotting talent. And you'll go far in this system. Believe me, I can tell. Now let's move on to tonight's topic—discipline."

He rose from his chair, grasped the lapels of his suit jacket with both hands, and pontificated.

"There are no bad students—only bad teachers! If you're having behavior problems, it's because you don't have your students under control!"

"That's exactly what Daddy says!" said Mary Fitzsimmens.

Dr. Van Dingle's lesson on discipline was very timely, if useless. But Van Dingle didn't trouble me much, as my expectations were at an all-time low.

Who did trouble me, and regularly, was Jimmy Crandle, the boy who had threatened his math teacher. Whenever I attempted to give a lesson, he would sit up on his desk, raise his voice above mine, and carry on with his personal business. Today was no exception.

"Would you please sit down, Jimmy. I need your attention."

"Cram it, Delano," he said, and turned aside with a grin, to the approval of his classmates.

"I don't want to call your father, but if you keep this up, I'll have no other choice."

"My father says you're a loser. He says anyone who's willing to work for less than fifty thou a year is a wimp."

The class began chanting in a singsong, "Wimp, wimp, wimp!"

I called Jimmy's father that evening.

"Mr. Crandle? This is Mr. Delano at Herbert Spencer. I'm having a problem with Jimmy."

"Are you the fag math teacher or the wimpy English one?"

"I'm your son's English teacher."

"You bother my boy one more time and I'm going to sue you!"

There was a sudden click, then a dial tone.

The next day, I shared my problem with Vice Principal Van Dingle. At first, he was attentive and seemed anxious to help.

"What do I do?" I concluded my story. "I've already called Jimmy's father and he threatened to sue me."

Van Dingle backed away from me as if he were afraid he might catch a contagious disease.

"Well, Mr. Delano. There are no bad students here at Herbert Spencer. There are, however, certain teachers who lack control over their classes."

"I'm willing to learn. What do I do if the boy continues to disrupt my class?"

He reached into his drawer and retrieved several forms.

"We only issue three of these per year to our teachers."

"What are they?"

"They're referral forms. You see, when a student misbehaves, and it does happen now and again, you fill out one of these forms and put it in my mailbox."

"What happens then?"

"Well, if the boy does it again, then you fill out another one and send it to me."

"Then what happens?"

121

"Then you have one form left. Be careful. It's your last."

"And after I use it?"

"Well, then you've used up all three forms. You are on your own at that point. I've done all I can. My hands are tied."

My discipline problem should have meant nothing to me, but in order to obtain my credential, I had to have a favorable report from my master-teacher. To appease her, I had to make an effort.

And it had spread beyond the one class. I was now confronted with problems in my third-period class. I assumed that the spitballs which flew through the air in my direction came from a kid named Michael.

"Did you do that, Michael?" I asked, debating whether or not to use a referral form.

"No, man. I swear on my mother's grave."

"That's right, Mr. Delano. He didn't do it," said one of the other students. "We can all testify in court that he didn't do it."

"Whoever I catch throwing spitballs is in real trouble."

Just then I saw her from the corner of my eye throw a large wad, squarely hitting an unpopular boy, Randy Newcomb, in the forehead.

The perpetrator was Malish Usnus, a pretty little blonde girl who was currently at the top of the honor roll.

"Malish, I saw that!"

"She didn't do it," said Randy.

"But I *saw* her do it."

"If you know what's good for you, Mr. Delano, you'll just forget it. She didn't do it."

"I saw her do it." The bell rang. "Randy, stay after class. I want to talk with you."

Randy was not like the other students at Herbert Spencer. He did not wear a fashionable down jacket, or Levi's cords, or expensive running shoes. Today he wore off-brand denim trousers and a faded black and blue flannel shirt that had seen many washings.

"Why did you say she didn't throw that spit wad?"

"Because my dad works for her dad at the feed store," he said, with an expression absent of any personality. "You don't know the Usnuses. They run the town. Mr. Usnus is the new county supervisor. He's a big shot lawyer. He owns half the dairies, the chicken ranches, and the feed store. Mr. Delano, Malish didn't do it."

"But Randy, it's not right. I saw her do it."

"You'll lose. So will my dad. She didn't do it."

Throughout my next class, the implication of what Randy had said bothered me. Never in my life had I felt such a sense of despair, not when Ashley gave me the clap, not even when I was about to go into combat and decided to shoot off my big toe.

It was lunchtime, but I had lost my appetite. I was sitting alone on a bench outside my classroom contemplating my future when I was approached by another teacher.

"My name's Ralph Martinelli. I teach social studies. How's it going?" he asked as we shook hands.

"I don't know. I think I might have made a mistake."

"Better to realize that now," he said, "than ten years down the road. Take my advice. No one else around here is going to give it to you straight, but if there's something else you can get into for a living, do it!"

"What do you mean?"

He cleared his throat, as if he were about to make a big speech.

"Well, let's put it this way. Half the teachers here are working on a real estate license, or they're selling Amway products. The few who aren't are kissing up to the administration so they can get in on the other side. And the kids? They're all doped up just like their parents." He smiled knowingly. "They don't tell you these things in college, do they? If they did, no one would go into teaching. But the fact is, over half these kids are from broken homes. They're living with their moms and their moms' boyfriends or girlfriends. The others should be from broken homes, but aren't. You ever meet any of the parents?"

I fumbled with my keys and said, "No, not yet."

"Well, be careful!" he warned. Then he looked at his watch. "Look, I've gotta run." He reached out to shake my hand again, smiling as if he had just made my day. "Nice meeting you, Delano. If you need any help or anything, just drop in. I'm in 217, just above the boiler room."

I was sure he was trying to help, but he hadn't. Then, to make matters worse, my master-teacher spotted me and walked up. She said she wanted to discuss some of the problems I was having.

"Eddie, teaching isn't for everybody," said Mrs. Van Dingle. "Perhaps you should consider some other line of work."

I was shattered. My future was collapsing.

"Have I done something wrong?"

"I want to show you something."

She led the way back to the classroom and pointed to one of the desks. Carved in the desk were the letters "M.U." and "This class sucks!"

"Eddie, this can't go on. You've got to catch the person who did this and put them on detention."

"I'll keep my eyes open."

"Also, I hate to tell you, but I'm hearing lots of complaints from parents that say that you do not give enough work."

"I've given them plenty of assignments. They just won't do them."

"You'll have to make the work more interesting."

"How do I make grammar interesting?"

"Let them substitute for grammar an essay on something they like. Instead of studying subject-verb agreement, let them write in their journals about how they feel about subject-verb agreement. Or instead of teaching them pronouns, let them draw a picture of what it's like to be a pronoun."

"Good idea," I lied.

"Give it a try, Eddie. Relax and enjoy it, or you will probably be asked to leave."

It was obvious that educating was the last thing any of these teachers or administrators at Herbert Spencer wanted. And the students didn't want to be taught, either. But I could hardly blame them. With an education, they would all have to become responsible for themselves.

Indeed, this was what made teaching an ideal career. No one would ever expect much from me because none of them really wanted to teach or learn anything. If I could just get through this trial period, I could then kick back and collect a check once a month.

That night as I lay in bed wide awake, the wheels of my imagination began to turn, until I came upon an educational concept that might make everybody happy. The next day I put it to the test.

"Okay, class. Since you won't work, or behave, let me make you a monetary offer." I immediately had their undivided attention.

"What if I give the person who writes the longest essay five bucks?"

"You cheap bastard," said Jimmy Crandle. "Fuck you!"

"Okay, ten bucks," I countered.

"Cram it, Delano," said Jimmy. "Make it twenty!"

"It's a deal," I said.

"What do we write about?" asked a little redheaded girl in the corner who was known across campus for granting sexual favors to the older boys.

"Whatever topic you want."

"Are you going to check our spelling?" inquired the son of one of our deputy sheriffs, cautiously.

"Heavens no. That's too much work."

"Are you going to grade us down for poor grammar or bad penmanship?" asked another boy, whose name I could never remember.

"Do you think I'm actually going to read these papers?"

"Can we do it for homework?"

"No. It's classwork. In fact, you can't take it home at all. I want you to do all your writing in class."

"How are you going tell whose paper is best?"

"I told you. I'll give twenty dollars to the student with the *longest* essay. And an A, too."

"Far-fucking-out!" Jimmy Crandle shouted. The students were laughing and giggling.

I had five classes, but it was worth a hundred bucks to keep them busy. And, indeed, they were happy with the assignment, and their attitude changed immensely. In fact, when my master-teacher returned to observe me, she was dumbfounded.

"My God, Delano. They're actually working! I've never seen anything like it. What did you do?"

"It's a motivational theory I'm working on."

"I'm impressed," she smiled. But then she seemed to remember something. "Have you caught the boy who has been carving on his desk?"

"No. But I have an idea who it is."

"Well, get to it, Eddie. This is where I really test your mettle."

Actually, I knew who had done it; the clue was in the initials. But I had to catch her in the act, so I rearranged the desks to entice my artist with a fresh canvas. If she did it once, she'd do it again.

125

16

Bad Karma

We were now into the fourth day of writing the longest essay. There had been some complaints, mostly of writer's cramp, but greed egged them on. There was an attempt by one of the boys to sabotage a rival's project. But aside from that, I was impressed by the Anglo-Saxon work ethic in action.

It was, however, in third period that day that I quietly crept up behind the culprit who I suspected of carving on the desk. At that very moment, I witnessed her carving her initials into the desk with a small penknife.

"So, Malish. You're the one who's been doing this."

"No! I didn't do it!" She quickly put away the knife.

"But I just saw you."

"I hate you! You shit-head!"

"You're staying after school on detention."

"No I'm not!" she said, standing defiantly with her hands on her hips. Then she grabbed her books and raged out of the class, slamming the door behind her.

I stood in front of my class bewildered. One of the boys in the front row smiled politely.

"You're dead meat now, Delano. She got rid of our fourth grade teacher the same way."

No more than half an hour passed before I was called to the office. Mrs. Usnus, Malish's mother, sat with Mr. Van Dingle. Politely, Van Dingle ushered me in and closed the door behind me.

"Eddie, Mrs. Usnus is here to talk with you."

"How do you do?" I offered my hand, but was rebuffed with a sneer.

"You know, ever since you've been my daughter's teacher, she's

126

been impossible to live with."

"I've only been her teacher for two weeks."

Van Dingle interjected, "Eddie, let Mrs. Usnus finish."

Mrs. Usnus continued, "She says that you're a lousy teacher."

This was true. How could I argue? I parried with a partial lie.

"I'm trying to do my best."

"Please, Eddie, don't interrupt," said Van Dingle.

"I can understand. You're a new teacher," said Mrs. Usnus curtly. "But today you went too far. How dare you try to keep my daughter after school! I'm a taxpayer!"

Smiling, Mr. Van Dingle clasped his hands.

"Eddie, what do you have to say for yourself?"

"Sir," then turning to Mrs. Usnus, "ma'am, your daughter was carving her initials on her desk with a penknife."

"That's impossible! My daughter would never do a thing like that!"

"Eddie," said Mr. Van Dingle, "I've known that young lady for years. I find it hard to believe she would do a thing like that."

"I caught her carving on the desk."

"Yes, yes," said Mr. Van Dingle, "but did you actually see her?"

"Yes, I did." Was the man hard of hearing?

"She says she didn't do it. Are there any witnesses?"

"The entire class."

He smiled to Mrs. Usnus and leaned back in his swivel chair. Then he clasped his hands comfortably behind his head and returned his attention to me.

"You can't put much stock in what the other kids say. Malish says that she didn't do it."

"Her initials are carved there. Would you like to see the desk?"

"Oh, Eddie, I don't think there's any need for that. Anybody could have carved her initials in that desk. More than likely it was that Randy Newcomb kid."

"I'm a taxpayer," Mrs. Usnus proudly announced again. "I pay your wages!"

"I'm not paid for student teaching. In fact I have to pay the college in order to do this."

"Well..." Mrs. Usnus was flustered. "One day you will be!"

"Now, now, Mrs. Usnus. Let's not get too upset," Van Dingle cooed, and then he turned to me. "Eddie, this is a nice community."

127

"Excuse me. Both of you!" I was getting angry. "You, Mrs. Usnus. Your daughter is a spoiled brat. I caught her red-handed carving her initials on—"

"Young man!" shouted Mr. Van Dingle, standing. "You don't talk to parents in my office like that!"

He folded his arms and sat back down. Once calmed, he smiled and continued condescendingly, "The parents, most of the parents here at Herbert Spencer Junior High, are concerned about their children. I'm sure you can see that."

"Not really."

"Mr. Delano! Please stop interrupting! You might as well know right now that you won't be student teaching here after today. Mrs. Usnus has taken the time to investigate you. As you might be aware, her husband is the new county supervisor. He used to be our district attorney. We've discovered something of an anomaly in your record."

"Yes, Mr. Delano," said Mrs. Usnus. "You're a communist! And I have proof." She produced a copy of an old newspaper photo. It was of the student riot.

"I can explain that, Mrs. Usnus. It was a case of mistaken identity."

"A likely story! We care too much about the welfare of our children to allow someone like you to undermine our values."

It was a moment of clarity. I knew exactly what to do. I pulled off my shoe and sock and threw them to the floor.

"Look at my foot!"

I was now sticking it in her face. And if having my foot in her face didn't shock her, the odor must have.

"I lost my toe in Vietnam so ungrateful people like you can have the freedom to call me a communist. A communist! Do you think a communist would give up his big toe for his country?"

Both of them were agape. I had them on the run.

"This is what I get for serving my country! This is what I get for losing my toe to keep this country safe from ungodly communists! You should be ashamed of yourselves!"

"I'm terribly sorry, Edward," said Mr. Van Dingle. "I—"

"Please, Mr. Delano," said Mrs. Usnus. "How can I ever make it up to you?"

"Forget it! It's too late for an abortion."

I left immediately after my confrontation with Van Dingle and Mrs. Usnus and drove home in a daze. When I got out of my car, I was only vaguely conscious of the green and white pickup truck parked in the driveway. Some part of me noted that I had never seen it before, but that was the extent of my awareness.

What was on my mind was that I had just deserted student teaching, and I was dreading facing Ashley with the fact. For some strange reason, I felt as if I were letting her down.

I walked into the house and thought an earthquake had hit. The walls were pounding, the floor was shaking, and the bed was squeaking.

Then I heard it: "Ram me! Ram me, Big Bull Daddy!"

I walked into the bedroom and froze at the sight of Ashley with another man. Directly, she became aware of my presence.

In a mixed state of ecstasy and embarrassment, she awkwardly grabbed for her clothing from a pile on the floor and pleaded desperately, "It's not what you think, Eddie. I can explain!"

The frightened middle-aged man with a balding crown held his hands up in the air.

"Hold on now, pardner! Ol' Chuck will be on his way. No reason to be hasty."

"Ram-me-Big-Bull-Daddy?" It was all I could say to him.

"That's what Sugar Britches calls me. But you can call me Chuck." He reached to shake my hand.

"Eddie, please let me explain," said Ashley. "I know it doesn't look good, but..."

I had only once been to Winston's condo. He had made it a matter of policy to keep his *protégés* out of his personal life, and I could hear from his tone of voice that he was not happy when the security guard at the gate relayed via the intercom my request to visit.

"Delano, what could be the problem?" he asked as he greeted me at the door. He didn't invite me inside.

"I'm desperate."

"The South Sea Islander thing?"

"No. I just left student teaching, and Ashley."

"Good for you. Now I've got to run."

"It's not all that great. I really need a friend right now."

"I suppose you do. Perhaps you should talk with someone."

"I'm talking with you."

"Yes, of course. Now, what is it you want to say?" He folded his arms impatiently and examined his wrist watch.

"I need a place to stay."

"Good luck."

"Do you mind if I stay with you?"

"Yes, of course."

"Yes I can stay?"

"No, yes I mind if you stay. It's not okay. I really value my privacy. In fact, there's a pretty young lady with no clothes on right this very minute waiting for me in my bedroom."

"I thought you were my friend."

"I am your friend. If I weren't, I would never have left that pretty naked lady to talk with you." He paused for a moment. "I don't want to sound heartless, Delano. But I'm afraid I have to return to my previous engagement."

"I need a friend."

"Haven't you made any other friends during your tenure at Del Norte?"

"Not really. A lot of the things you taught me have made me pretty antisocial."

"You're blaming that on me? I merely recognized certain sociopathic tendencies in you. All I did was to help you blossom. Now you want to dump your problems on me?"

"I thought you were my friend, Winston."

"You should have gotten a dog. I hear they're very loyal. Speaking of dogs, whatever happened to that primitive roommate of yours? Why don't you give him a call? Now, I've got to return to business, if you don't mind."

I was shaken with the sudden realization of my situation. Winston assumed a bored attitude.

"No hard feelings, Delano. It's nothing personal." He yawned wistfully into the back of his hand. "I just don't need any extra baggage, especially when I'm about to get laid."

It didn't happen immediately, but eventually the words "primitive roommate" finally sank in. I found Sam's map under a pile of papers in my glove compartment and drove up towards the Sugar Loaf where he lived.

Sam greeted me and invited me inside.

"What brings you up to this neck of the woods?" he asked.

Sitting at his kitchen table, I recounted the events of the day.

"Bummer, man. Especially the thing with Ashley. Must be bad karma. Better now than in your next life."

Sam was silent for a few moments, thinking.

"You know, I didn't wanna say anything at the time, Eddie," he said with resignation. "But considering how things have turned out, you might as well know."

Then he stopped himself, reconsidering.

"What, Sam?" I prodded him.

"Never mind. Maybe it's really best not to say."

"Sam, you better tell me."

"Well, you remember when I invested my money in psychedelic commodities with Hog? You know, just after my worm plantation failed me? Remember I told you 'bout a high-class chick I almost got it on with in a biker bar?"

"Vaguely."

"Well..." he stopped himself again. "Ah, never mind."

"Sam, tell me!"

"Well, the girl I almost did it with..."

"Come on, spit it out."

"It was..." he swallowed, "Ashley."

"Ashley!" My mind was racing; suddenly the whole ugly picture became clear. "Why didn't you say something when you picked up the dead horse? You recognized her, didn't you?"

"Well, she seemed different with you. More stable. I figured she must have sowed up her wild oats and was settled down. But there's something else I gotta say. Hog said she was kinda weird—real weird."

"How did Hog come to know her?"

"From his brother, Kevin. A real animal type. The kinda guy who gives felons a bad name. Anyways, Kevin and her used to get it on—on the pool table when the bar was closed."

"This would have been helpful information, Sam."

"Well, I guess I can tell you the rest. Hog says she spent some time in a nut house. I bet it has a lot to do with reading books. Remember I told you about the dude I knew who got a brain tumor 'cause he read too much? Betcha that's what happened to her."

"I figured she was crazy," I said despondently.

"Well, if you already knew she was crazy..." Sam began, but he kindly refrained from stating the obvious. "Listen, how 'bout a beer?" He got up and moved to the refrigerator.

I looked at Sam with a newfound respect. There was a strength in him that I had never realized he had.

"Sam, I was wondering if I could stay here for a while."

"For sure, man." He handed me a beer and added, "I consider you my very best friend."

Sam claiming me as his very own best friend might have struck me as funny a day earlier. But in light of all that had just happened, I realized that this goofy-looking flower child with his moronic grin and bloodshot eyes had a bigger heart than anyone else I'd met in the past few years. I had believed my awareness of things to be superior to Sam's, and now I was learning a lesson in humility from him.

This had been a day of reckoning. I discovered that teaching was not in my future, that my girlfriend was hopelessly unfaithful, and that the one person I had come to count on over the years wasn't much of a friend at all.

But then there was Sam, and he was a friend.

17

The Grace of God

Six months passed. In that time, I had managed to fix up an old rusted silver trailer next to Sam's garage.

From the kitchen table in the trailer, I could look out the small window and see the redwood forest ascending from the river up Sugar Loaf Ridge. In the late afternoon, the shadow of the ridge would fall upon the trailer and this side of the valley. It was an ideal location for someone who wanted to be lost.

For the first couple of months, I was genuinely incapacitated. In the middle of the night my arm would fall where Ashley used to be, and I would wake with a sudden start and then painfully realize that it was over. No more free rent.

In retrospect, I understood that sooner or later something had to give. Indeed, I might have ended up marrying Ashley, and then we might have broken up after we had been together a longer time, so it could have been much worse. No, as hard as it had been discovering the truth, it was for the best in the long run.

Of course, I'd lost the prospect of ever becoming a teacher. But that was the way I wanted it. I did have some money left over from all my grants and scholarships, not to mention my small but appreciated government disability pension for the loss of my toe, and Sam was charging me only fifty bucks a month because I was his best friend.

As for women, I decided to revert to my one-percent theory. Every sunny day I went to the river and pretended to read while scamming on the girls who were sunning themselves.

One day as I sat on the sandy riverbank, Ashley appeared suddenly at my side. When I looked up, the sun blinded me, and I could not immediately tell who it was. For a moment, all I could see were the pleasant, shapely curves of a woman. Then she moved in front of me, and my anticipation withered.

"What a surprise," she said. "I didn't know you came up to this part of the river." She smiled timidly. "How've you been?"

I could not answer.

"I never hear from you. You still mad?" she asked with trepidation. "Ed-dieee," she crooned. An awkward moment of silence passed. "I've missed you."

I looked away from her and fixed my attention on the tall redwood trees across the river.

"You don't know how sorry I am," she said.

"It won't do you any good." The furthest thing from my mind was rekindling a relationship with her.

Her aristocratic fingers played with her car keys.

"What won't do me any good?" she asked innocently.

"Following me out here."

Slightly annoyed, she said, "I'm not following you." Then a tear rolled down her cheek, and her eyes quickly became red and puffy. "I'm sorry. Give me another chance. I love you."

I held back from laughing.

"What about Chuck?"

Looking at the ground between us, she replied, "I'm not seeing him anymore. He disgusts me. Turns out he's a transvestite. I caught him trying on my panties and bra."

"I'd think that would turn you on."

A hurt expression filled her face as she struggled to defend herself. "It was awful. Chuck is so sick! Don't you think?"

"I don't care if he fucks horses, Ashley."

She dropped the car keys.

"Ashley," I said, as I picked up her keys, "it was a big mistake for both of us. We were both using each other, and it was best we stopped it when we did."

"I wasn't using you."

She was lying.

"Fine. You weren't using me. I was using you."

I was not lying for a change.

"You bastard!"

"Yes," I said, handing her the keys.

She turned to walk away, and then she remembered something.

"By the way, the vice principal and a bunch of kids at Herbert Spencer Junior High have been calling for you."

"Please do not forward my address or phone number to them or anyone else," I said coldly.

"But, Eddie. I don't have your address or phone number."

"Perfect!"

"You don't have to be so hostile!" And with that, she plodded away angrily through the sand.

I lay back down in the warm sun and felt a strange calm wash over my body. I felt anything but hostile. After some contemplation, I realized the extent of my good fortune. I was over Ashley. I was free.

Another few months passed, and I was at peace. I fished, gardened, met some new girls, and almost read a book. I was working on a new level of consciousness.

Then one day I was just waking up from a short nap on the sandy riverbank when I saw Sam in his old truck cruising up the dirt road next to the river. I sensed something bad was about to happen.

He left the truck and marched in my direction. When he reached me, I saw he had a serious expression on his face.

"Say, man. Got some bad news. Your mom just called. Your dad had a heart attack. Your mom says she needs you."

"When did it happen?"

"She didn't say. Man, more bad karma," he said sympathetically. "I guess you'll be goin' home. How long do you think you'll be gone?"

"I don't know." I felt dread like the closing of a coffin.

Once back in Southern California, my first stop was at the butcher shop. I bought a large, meaty soup bone. Then I drove down my parents' street and parked my car out of sight of their home. As I walked up, I spotted Oscar, that retarded asshole of a dog, sprawled on the porch. Though he could not see me, I could tell by the way he lifted his nose to the breeze that he scented the bone.

135

I crawled along the hedge that bordered my parents' house and I tossed the bone onto the driveway. The sound alerted him, and he rose to an attack position. His nose directed him to the bone.

As he viciously chewed it, I ran up to the front door and rang the doorbell.

"Who is it?"

"It's me, Mom," I said excitedly.

"Who?"

"Eddie! Open the door, quick!"

"Okay, Eddie."

"Mom, hurry!"

"Hold your horses, Son." I heard the clanking of metal, the jiggling of a chain, and the sliding of a bolt.

Suddenly, Oscar was upon me.

"Grrrrr! Rooof, rooof!"

He went for my ankles first. Then he was at the seat of my pants.

"Please, Mom. Hurry!" I was terrified.

I heard another bolt slide and the fumbling of more chains. Oscar renewed his attack on me with even more vigor. I turned to kick the dog in the mouth, but he grabbed my foot and bit down hard.

"Mom, please hurry!" I was in pain.

The door opened; Oscar's ears went limp, his tail began to wag, and his biting turned to licking.

"Yes, that's right, Oscar. Eddie's home. Boy, does that dog love you!" Then she noticed my irritated condition. "Eddie, you're going to end up in the hospital just like your father if you don't learn how to relax."

"Oscar was attacking me!"

"You haven't changed a bit, Eddie. I don't know why you never liked Oscar. You're beginning to sound just like the neighbors. I just don't understand why everyone dislikes that poor lovable puppy," she said, leading the way inside.

"The dog is vicious! You're lucky no one has ever sued you because of him." I took a deep breath and said, "I don't mean to change the subject, but how is Dad?"

A worried look filled her face. "The Lord is testing us." She could not seem to muster the strength to tell me more.

We walked into the living room and sat on the sofa.

"How did it happen?"

"Well, you know his weight problem. And he's been worrying so much lately."

"About what?"

"Communists. The ones on TV. And the new neighbors. Your father says they're all communists."

"How does he know the neighbors are communists?"

"They jog."

"That's ridiculous."

"It's true, Eddie. Your father says that fitness is a communist conspiracy to ruin the garment industry, and then the healthcare industry. He says that's how they took over Poland. They ruin one industry at a time."

"Are you sure he didn't have a nervous breakdown?"

She shrugged her shoulders and told me I could see for myself soon enough.

"Son," my father said as he recognized me. He motioned for me to come closer, then whispered, "Son, could you do a dying man a favor?"

Fear gripped me for a moment. "You're not gonna die," I said.

"You too? You're all trying to humor me."

"No, I'm not. It's the truth. If you lose weight, you can be healthy again."

"Son, just do me one last favor. I've written down something here. I want you to look at it."

I thought that it must be a last will and testament, given the way he guarded its secrecy. I silently read what he had neatly printed on the paper: "Get me some pork ribs. And a large pizza with pepperoni and sausage."

I looked at him, and he had a tear in his eye.

"Please, Son. For a dying man. I can't stand it. All I've had is this low calorie stuff. It's killing me." And with those few words, he dozed off.

My father's doctor, who had quietly stepped into the room while my father and I had been talking, put his hand on my shoulder.

"Perhaps you ought to leave before your father wakes up and talks you into buying him any more junk food." He smiled, and then added, "Yesterday he bribed an orderly into bringing him a burrito and a half-gallon of strawberry ice cream."

"When can he go home?"

"Maybe next week. We're trying to squeeze as much as we can out of his policy. The only problem is that your father has made a very quick recovery."

"So it wasn't a major heart attack?"

"Good heavens, no. It was angina, but your father insisted that it was a heart attack. And to speak quite frankly, Mr. Delano, when we found out how extensive his insurance policy was, naturally we agreed with him." He paused before adding, "It's my professional opinion that he's a nervous wreck. He worries too much about politics. He actually insists that the Boston Marathon is a communist conspiracy."

"Is there anything you can do for him?"

"Yes, we've already put him on Valium. He's taken to them like a fish to water. You'd think he couldn't live without them."

"Aren't they addictive?"

"Yes, they are," he said with a chuckle. "I've had to double his dose this week. But don't worry about a thing, Mr. Delano. I put my own wife on them years ago, and they've worked wonders."

"Your wife?"

"Yes, my wife. She used to drive me nuts, but she's a much happier person now. A wonderful woman." He looked at his watch. "Well, I've got to go now. I have exploratory surgery in a few minutes. We're examining someone else's insurance policy."

He checked off something on the clipboard at the end of my father's bed and then strolled away down the hall whistling.

"Mom, I don't think Dr. Saunders knows what he's doing."

"Now you're a medical expert! I happen to know that Dr. Saunders is a wonderful doctor. He's a fine Christian. He attends our church regularly."

"I don't see how going to church proves he's a good doctor."

"You should try going to church once in a while. Even your friend Conrad started attending."

"Conrad's going to church?"

"Yes, and he always asks about you. You should be more like Conrad, Eddie. He's such a nice boy. And so is his wife. You should look for someone like her and get married and settle down."

138

"I'm not sure I'll ever get married, Mom."

"That's ridiculous," she replied. "You should go visit Conrad after we get home. You'll see."

Reluctantly, I took her advice and visited Conrad the next day. To be honest, I was curious as to why he had started going to church. That was unlike him.

He greeted me at the gate to his apartment building.

"I'd invite you in, but Carry still hates you."

"I have this way with women."

"So how did college turn out?"

"You were right. It was a memorable experience."

"What was it like?" he asked with an envious gleam in his eye.

"Well, lots of women, lots of drugs, and no responsibilities."

"Too bad you graduated. Now you have to go out and find a job and join the rest of us working stiffs."

"I don't know, Conrad. There's always graduate school."

"Well, I can see it's done you wonders. You seem much more relaxed and—"

He was interrupted by a terrifying, shrill scream.

"Conrad!"

His face turned ashen white.

"Gotta go!"

A beastly, overweight woman stood in the doorway to his apartment. "Conrad! Get your ass in here, now!"

It was Carry, my old girlfriend—Conrad's wife!

Solemnly, he said good bye. Then, shoulders slumped and hands in his pockets, he walked dutifully away.

There but for the grace of God...

18

Little Blue Friends

We celebrated the day my father returned from the hospital by going to a restaurant called Fat Boy's Famous Barbecue and Buffet.

"I got a real craving for ribs," said my father as we pulled into the parking lot of Fat Boy's. "Big, juicy pork ribs."

"No ribs, Lazlo. Chicken or fish. You've got to watch your cholesterol!"

"Okay, we'll compromise. Barbecued chicken. That does sound good. A big, juicy barbecued chicken, smothered in Fat Boy's secret barbecue sauce. Hmm, umm!"

"Not an entire chicken, Lazlo. No more than a breast."

"Okay, a big juicy breast of chicken," said my father turning to me with a wink.

My father was the size of man who made restaurant owners with all-you-can-eat specials wince. When we walked in, I spotted Mr. Reynolds, the legendary Fat Boy himself, and I saw him roll his eyeballs up into their sockets as my dad reconnoitered the display of food at the buffet table. It was brimming over with an array of deep-fried and broiled meats, platters of creamed vegetables, and bowls full of various gravies.

Mr. Fat Boy's relief came when my mother dragged my father from the buffet, scolding him.

"Count your calories and cholesterol. Do you hear me, Lazlo? Calories and cholesterol!"

We were seated in an out-of-the-way section and were quickly given menus. My father's eyes occasionally lifted above the menu, exploring the display at the buffet table the way a sex-crazed man explores bikinis at the beach.

Unfortunately for him, my mother, ever vigilant, would reward his interest with a hostile glare, and he would sheepishly return his eyes to the menu.

Shortly after we ordered, my father said, "There was a guy in the hospital. Shared my room. I swear the doctor said he had an enlarged wallet. Maybe I was dreaming it. Maybe it was a joke. Ever hear of anything like that when you were in college, Eddie?"

"No, can't say I have."

"The guy said he felt fine. Said he never felt better in his whole life. Goes in to see the doctor for a check up, and the next thing you know, he's in the hospital. I wonder sometimes if those doctors know what they're doing."

"Take another blue tablet, Lazlo. The doctor said that when you start asking silly questions, you should take a blue tablet."

"I like the blue ones. They're very nice."

As we waited for our food, my parents asked me questions about my life in college. I had possibly made a mistake by telling them a little too much over the years.

"Explain it to me again, Son," said my father. "You received a scholarship for being a South Sea Islander?"

"It's real complicated, Dad."

"Things sure are different these days."

"Tell me about the girl you were going around with, Eddie," said my mother.

"Oh, I don't see her anymore. It was kind of a mistake."

"You know, Eddie," she said. "You'll have to settle down one day. I'll bet she was a lovely young lady."

"Of course. Very moral," I said sarcastically.

"So that probably disappointed *you*. I know you, Eddie. You think you're too good for everybody. You'd better get humble or you'll find yourself all alone in this world."

I thought about Conrad, shivered inwardly, and said nothing.

"Whatever became of your student teaching, Son?" asked my father.

"It was, uh, not exactly what I thought it would be. I don't think they like disabled veterans."

"Well, teaching's a pretty good job," he said. "Steady work. But as long as you find something you like. You think you'll find a job here now? We were kind of hoping you'd move back. You could see all your old friends again. Wouldn't you like that?"

141

"I wouldn't mind that." Through the bombsight of a B-52. Among other things, my brief visit with Conrad had convinced me that if I had any friends at all, they were in Northern California. I thought about Sam, and Alice.

Once the food arrived, my father succumbed to a meditative state of oneness with his stomach. It was like watching a priest lost in prayer, or a Hindu preparing to levitate.

As if to compensate for my father's voracious appetite, my mother cautiously dipped her fork into her salad dressing before spearing each individual leaf of lettuce.

When my father finished his chicken, I noticed him eyeballing the last of my ribs. My mother, who had observed my father's new-found interest in my dinner, delicately wiped the corner of her mouth with her napkin and spoke up.

"Don't even think about it, Lazlo!" She nodded to the waitress and asked for the bill. "Let's go home."

"Yes, dear," said my father.

On the drive home, I was pensive. The questions about college had reminded me of more than just my recent setbacks; they had brought back a lot of fond memories, as well. I longed for the life, however shabby, that I had made for myself. I remembered fondly the view of the woods and river from my trailer.

The following morning, I awoke earlier than my parents and rode my bicycle to the corner market for some milk. I returned home just as my father entered the kitchen. I placed the milk on the table. I was still slightly out of breath from the ride and from eluding Oscar.

"You've been jogging! Don't lie to me! You've been jogging. My very own son!"

"No I haven't. I rode my bicycle to the market for some milk."

"Lazlo," said my mother, handing him an amber plastic bottle. "Take one of these."

"My very own son is a communist!" he said, taking the bottle from my mother.

He shook several blue tablets into the palm of his hand and then swallowed them down with a glass of water. Soon, my father was very relaxed and eased himself down in front of the TV to watch a rerun of "Maverick."

Several hours passed quietly, and then the phone rang. My mother became agitated with the person on the phone and started shouting. "Oscar wouldn't do a thing like that! Besides, I happen to know that he is right here at home!" She turned to me and said, "Get Oscar, right now!" She put the phone back to her ear and continued to argue.

Oscar was nowhere to be found. When I returned, my mother replayed the conversation to me. Oscar had attacked the neighbor's son while he was riding his bike. The neighbors were seeing a lawyer.

"Mom, I told you Oscar was a troublemaker!"

"Let's see what your father has to say."

She called to him. My father turned his head in our direction, wearing a silly little smile as he sang along off-key, "...the professor and Marianne, here on Gilligan's Isle."

"Lazlo! Snap out of it!"

"That Gilligan! What a crack up," said my father.

"Lazlo, the neighbors are suing us because of Oscar."

"Our Oscar?"

"Mom, just find a good lawyer and chances are it will never go to court."

"Son, you worry too much," said my father in a sedated voice.

"I'd find a good lawyer right now," I said.

"Oh, Eddie," said my father. "I used to think like that. Take one of these yellow tablets. They're good. No, wait. Take one of these blue ones. They're better."

"If this family prayed together, things like this wouldn't happen," said my mother. Then she looked at me accusingly. "It's because of your negative attitude, Eddie, that God is punishing us."

My father picked up the phone book and listlessly thumbed through the yellow pages until he found Attorneys at Law.

"Abbot, Allen—Attorney. Sounds like a good one."

"He must be the best, Lazlo. His name is the first one on the list."

"That's because it's in alphabetical order," I said.

"Eddie," my mother said in a sad, plaintive voice. "You always find fault with your parents."

"Look," I pointed to the listing. "It says he's a divorce lawyer. Maybe he doesn't handle this kind of case."

"Oh, Mr. Perry Mason," said my father in a drug-induced whimsy. "Smart-aleck college kid goes away to school. Now you know more than your mother and father."

"Honor thy mother and father, Eddie. That's what the Good Book says."

"Okay, have it your way. Abbot Allen is probably as good a lawyer as you might find anywhere."

There was a metallic clank at the front-door mail drop, and my mother left to investigate.

"I don't understand anything anymore, Eddie," said my father. "The world used to be such a simple place, and then it all got so confusing. What the hell," he added with a whimsical smile.

"Eddie," said my mother, returning. "There's something here for you. It looks official."

It was a letter from Del Norte State College, forwarded to my parents' address. It had been stamped several times and the envelope was worn and soiled.

"Open it," said my mother. "What's it say?"

I read it aloud.

> *Dear Mr. Edward Delano:*
>
> *Due to the confusion and obvious misunderstanding of a certain unfortunate event you experienced during your student teaching, and reconsidering your unique success at Herbert Spencer Junior High School, on behalf of the Department of Education at Del Norte State College, we hereby award you with your Single Subject Credential.*
>
> *In order to complete your paper work, please bring this letter to room TT-635, and a check made payable to the State of California for the sum of twenty-five dollars.*
>
> > *Sincerely yours,*
> > *Dr. F. Van Dingle*
> > *Chairman, Education Department*
>
> *P.S.*
>
> *Vice Principal Richard Van Dingle is deeply moved by how much your students miss you. Everyday they ask, "Where's our teacher? We want Mr. Delano." I just want*

to add, Eddie, we've never seen kids so mo-
tivated. In spite of impending cut backs, Vice
Principal Van Dingle thinks he can hire you
for next fall.

"Son! We're so proud of you!" said my mother.

"It's not what you think."

"You're too modest, Eddie," said my father. "You refused to talk about your war experiences when you returned from Vietnam, and now you keep this success from us."

"We're so proud of you, Son," said my mother again. "While other parents are worried sick over their ungrateful children who go to college, use dope, and come down with venereal diseases, our little Eddie modestly and quietly goes about winning praise from none other than the chairman of the education department!"

"It's not what it seems, Mom. I'm not all that perfect."

"Good ol' Delano modesty," said my father.

"Well, it looks like you're going to have to go back up north and take care of business," said my mother.

This was the break I was looking for.

"You're sure you don't need any more help around here?" I asked.

"We're capable of taking care of ourselves," said my father, still smiling. "As long as I have my little blue friends, everything will turn out fine."

19

Triumph

Returning to Northern California seemed like a sensible thing to do. I liked living at Sam's place in the redwoods. It was peaceful there, and I could take my time to decide what I wanted to do. I could pursue my credential, or maybe I'd enroll in the M.A. program at Del Norte and pick up where Winston had left off. There were a lot of possibilities.

It sounded simple when I thought it through on the long drive north, but Sam was about to complicate my life. He was sitting on the porch when I drove up.

He greeted me with a grimace.

"I got busted while you were gone, dude," he said with a note of resentment in his voice.

The ensuing silence asked the next question, and he offered an answer.

"Yeah. Real heavy duty," he said, as if that were all he needed to say for me to understand what had happened.

I didn't know what to say. The silence that followed became uncomfortable.

"There's something fishy going on," he said, lifting his head up and back. There was accusation in his posture. Then, as if he were making the final point, "Things are not what they appear to be."

"What are you talking about? What happened?"

"I went to score some real righteous stuff, man. Stuff coming down from Humbolt. Heavy duty, ya know?"

I nodded my head and he continued.

"Anyways, to make a long story short, just as I gave this doofus dude my dinero, a bunch of cops jumped out of the bushes and put me in the poky!" He hung his head low.

"I'm sorry, Sam. Can I help you with anything?"

"You bet you can," he said, looking at me directly in the eyes. "Something here ain't right, Eddie. The cops didn't care that much about the pot."

I was frightened by Sam's demeanor. He read my fear and it fueled him on.

"They knew everything about Hog, Baba What's-His-Face, and all those student radicals you used to hang out with." The accusation loomed larger and darker in his eyes. "They knew all about you!"

"Me! What the hell did I do?"

"That's what I want to know, Eddie."

"Don't ask me, Sam. I'm just as puzzled as you are. You don't think I had anything to do with you getting busted, do you?"

"Indirectly, yeah! The cops would never have had the slightest interest in me if it weren't for you. They set me up to get to you!"

"Why were they after me? I didn't do anything."

"They say you got this outstanding warrant, and that you're a subversive."

"A warrant? A subversive!"

"You're a slippery hombre, Delano. They said they almost had you behind bars, but you gave them the old flimflam."

"I don't know what you're talking about."

"Why didn't you ever tell me about trying to take over the library?" He was growing angrier as he spoke. "What a dumb-ass thing to do!"

"I have no intentions of taking over the library." But as I spoke, I remembered the meeting at Fernie's with the New People's Army.

"And who the hell is this Ee-deee Ah-men?"

"Idi Amin? He's some cannibal I read about in *Time* magazine."

"Why would anyone wanna name the library after someone that no one has ever heard of?"

"Your guess is as good as mine. Look, Sam. I didn't get mixed up with a bunch of radicals. I wouldn't have spent two minutes in their company, but there was this good-looking redhead with them."

"That explains it all," he said in mock relief. "You think with your dick, Eddie! I hate to tell you, but being that I'm your best friend and all, I gotta give it to you straight. You got yourself in a couple of jams since I've known you because you didn't know that your pecker ain't your brain!"

147

"She was really good-looking."

"That's no excuse for not using [ ] head to illustrate the point. "So you got yourself involved [ ] bunch of subversives. What in the world did they want with the library?"

"Hell, I don't know. In fact, they didn't even like me."

I started to describe the sequence of events, but he wasn't listening to me. He must have gone a million miles away.

"Eddie!" he blurted out from behind a blind stare. "They're gonna put me in jail if I don't play ball! I gotta help them put the bikers away."

"That sounds pretty complicated. And dangerous."

"You're telling me! You know what Hog and his friends will do to me if they find out I set them up?"

He looked to be suffering from intestinal gas, which more than likely meant he was turning the unpleasant idea over in his brain. Then he resumed his line of reasoning.

"You gotta understand something. It's not my idea. But the cops told me they want you in on this. I don't know the radicals. I only know Hog."

"What do they want you to do?"

"They want *us* to set up a drug deal. An exchange for explosives, or something. And on that Baba guy's ranch. The bikers, the Babas, and the radicals." He paused again to examine my reaction, and then added, "If you don't cooperate, they're gonna bust you sooner or later. That's what they told me to tell you."

"Not me. You're barking up the wrong tree."

"They said they'll drop the warrant on you, if you go along."

"That warrant is bogus. I got it because of a broken bicycle reflector."

Sam got up, moved to the porch steps and sat down dejectedly, and I realized that his dilemma was now mine. I felt as if someone had kicked me in the gut. There went my future. I could forget about the teaching credential, taking Winston's place, the M.A. program, the coeds, the sexual favors for better grades, and the bribes.

Sam must have been reading my mind.

"I don't like this any more than you do, but if we don't go along with the cops, they're gonna screw us good."

"But, Sam. I don't know how to set people up for cops. I don't

148

know anything about dealing drugs, or explosives, or Baba Rama. And the New People's Army hates me."

"The cops say it'll be easy. They say they got this informer who's working on the inside. All they want us to do is arrange a deal. They want us to get all three groups together."

"I'm not sure I want to do this, Sam. I don't care if Hog wants to smoke dope, or even sell it. I don't care about Baba Rama, either. If people want to be stupid, they have a right to be stupid."

"I don't like it, either, but they've got us over a barrel."

"Let me sleep on it."

I tried to sneak out in the middle of the night, but Sam was wide awake.

"Where you going, dude?" he asked as he turned on the porch light in front of the house.

"I had an urge for a burrito."

"You need to pack up all your stuff just to get a burrito?"

"I was figuring on getting it in Mexico."

"Go ahead and go. I can't stop you from running away from trouble."

"Look, I'm not that noble, Sam. I have a strong survival instinct, and it's telling me that I better get the hell out of here."

"Your warrant ain't gonna go away."

"I'm sure the cops have better things to worry about."

"I'm sure you're right," he said, resigned to his fate. He dropped his shoulders and cast a worried glance aside.

He was always easy to feel sorry for. I chose him as a roommate because I felt sorry for him. But I had never seen him so low. Even when his worm plantation failed him, he didn't look like this.

"Okay, damn it! It's against my better judgment, but if it'll make you happy..."

He was thrilled.

"You won't regret this, dude. Really."

"I'm already beginning to have second thoughts."

We drove to the sheriff's department the following morning. Sam had called ahead and spoken with one of the cops who had busted him and said we were coming in.

149

In front of the county courthouse just across the parking lot from the sheriff's station, some of Baba Rama's followers were making their rounds selling flowers. It was common knowledge that they would start off each day at the civic center and then move on to another location where there was a lot of foot traffic, like the shopping center or the college.

I strained my eyes searching for Alice, hoping to see her in that group. For a moment, I thought I recognized her, but it could not have been Alice. The girl I was looking at was too thin and sickly-looking to be her.

Sam knew what I was doing and said, "Did you see her?"

"Who?" I asked, trying to hide my concern.

"You know who. Alice!"

"No, I didn't see her. You know, Sam, I should have stopped her from joining those morons."

"Yep. You should have."

We were soon escorted to an empty office where we waited for a Detective Ford. Some time passed.

"Looks like he's a no-show, Sam. Let's get out of here."

Just then Ford walked in. He was tall and had a military haircut. In the army, I had seen hundreds of faces just like his on officers and NCOs—faces chiseled by regimented discipline, self-denial, and self-righteous indignation.

"So you're Eddie Delano," he said with a cruel smile. "We've been looking for you for a long time."

"Yeah, I'm a real danger to society."

"You've had an outstanding warrant for almost five years."

"For a broken bicycle reflector."

"No one cares about your bicycle reflector. You failed to appear, so that ticket went to warrant. And that's serious."

"Give me a break. Don't you people have better things to do?"

"As a matter of fact, we do. And you're going to help us. Or you're going to jail."

He explained it very clearly, twice. In two days, Wednesday, I was to talk to the leaders of the New People's Army and Sam was to talk to Hog and the bikers. We were to set up the actual exchange for the following morning, Thursday, at Baba Rama's.

"Could you say that again?" Sam asked.

So Ford repeated the plan again, concluding, "We want the

bikers to exchange stolen C-4 explosives with Baba Rama for high-grade marijuana, and the radicals to exchange money for the C-4 explosives. As soon as the exchange is made, we move in and put an end to Mr. Rama's little cult, stop the radicals from blowing themselves up, and chase the bikers out of the county for good."

"Okay, gotcha," said Sam. "But why do we have to do it at Mr. Baba's place?"

"We want all of this to occur in one spot at one time. That way we can get them all with one quick kill."

"Okay, gotcha. But it sounds like bad karma, dude."

"Karma doesn't have anything to do with it! Besides, if we can't pull this off, you and Delano go to jail."

I joined in with Sam, "Okay, gotcha!"

Just then Ford's partner entered and gave him a look that said there was other business to take care of.

"Is there anything else you need to know, Sam?" asked Ford with a strained face.

"I don't know. I'm still a little confused."

"Get the hell out of here! I'll come by tomorrow morning and write it down for you!" Ford turned to his partner and said, "That kid is dumber than a door knob."

"Which one?" his partner replied dryly.

I was not thrilled with my predicament. But as we left the building, I felt some degree of relief that the warrant for my arrest would be dropped and that I could start over with a clean record.

Sam and I crossed the parking lot towards his truck.

"Who do you think it is that the cops have on the inside?" I asked Sam when we reached the truck. "I was under the impression that it was one of the radicals."

"They said something before about someone at the college working for them," he said, stepping into the cab.

"It's a damn shame they're gonna bust that good-looking red-head," I said, closing the truck door behind me.

"There you go again!" Sam assumed a superior attitude as he gunned the engine. "Pecker for brains!"

We had pulled into traffic and were heading for home when a yellow van slowly passed us and moved into a left-turn lane. I recalled seeing it in the parking lot at the courthouse. It was now loaded with Baba Rama's disciples.

Suddenly, a look of recognition filled Sam's face.

"It's Alice!"

Sam made a sudden, wide swing across the road, nearly causing an accident.

"What the hell are you doing?"

"Alice! Eddie, it was Alice in the van! If we don't get her away from Baba Rama's people, she could end up getting busted!"

We got turned around and spotted the yellow van as it pulled onto the freeway. Sam sped up.

"But what are we going to do when we catch up with them?" I asked.

"Rescue Alice! What else?"

Of course. What else? What was I thinking? Sam was right. We had to catch up with them.

"Faster, Sam!"

For an hour we trailed the van south until we eventually found ourselves at the airport. This was one of their favorite spots for hustling small change. We followed the van into the airport garage. From a safe distance, we tracked the group up to the arrival and departure gates. All the while, I looked for Alice among them.

They began selling flowers to travelers. The tall, bald leader never allowed his charge to stray far from his sight.

Sam spotted Alice before I did. She looked frail and tired. She *was* the sickly-looking girl I had seen at the courthouse.

We walked right up behind her. Sam grabbed my arm and whispered, "Eddie, get her!" And he shoved me in front of her.

"Sir, would you like to buy a flower?"

"Alice! It's me, Eddie!"

"Eddie, would you like to buy a flower?"

"Alice, snap out of it!"

Her eyes seemed to focus. Then they opened wide.

"Eddie Delano? It's you!" She threw her arms around me. Then we stared at each other—for only a fraction of a second, but an eternity passed between us.

"Eddie, get me out of here!"

"Run, Alice!" I said, pushing her towards Sam. "Don't look back!"

I crouched and turned to see if anyone was following her. Suddenly, the leader of the group ran directly into me. It must have looked as if I had deliberately blocked him with my shoulder. The truth was that it was simply a stroke of dumb luck.

I had knocked the wind out of him. He collapsed and hit the floor. I was only stunned for a moment before I took off in a sprint and caught up with Sam and Alice. We ran across the street, dodging traffic in a frantic ballet done to the sounds of horns blowing in pro-test and cars screeching to a halt in order to avoid hitting us.

We made our way back to Sam's truck, jumped into the cab, and fled through the garage and out the exit. We were safe.

I exchanged a look of giddy triumph with Sam, and then we both looked at Alice. She was staring up at me.

"You saved me, Eddie."

I put my arm around her, and she leaned into me and clutched my hand.

Sam appeared to be touched by the image we made. The look on his face was of a different kind of triumph. He smiled at us warmly.

"Man, am I hungry!" he said, probing us. "Wha'da ya say?"

Alice perked up immediately.

"I'm *so* hungry, Eddie. Do you know a good place that has good hamburgers or hot dogs?"

She looked up at me playfully. I was smiling from ear to ear.

20

En Tedium

Rescuing Alice from the clutches of maniacal cultists had a major disadvantage. She and Sam both now thought I was a hero, and though I relished the idea at first, I quickly realized they were thinking that I was a lot braver than I really was—a lot braver—and that helping the cops bust everyone should be just a matter of routine.

The truth was, I was scared shitless. In spite of all the attention Alice gave me, I was almost in a state of nervous exhaustion just thinking about it.

When Detective Ford showed up at the cabin the next morning, I felt the way I did just before I decided to shoot off my toe.

"Well, boys, the day of reckoning is upon us."

Sam and I looked at each other for support. We both swallowed hard and turned our attention to Ford, who had a sadistic smile.

"Sam, you are going to take a trip tomorrow to the other side of the valley. You're going to Hog's place. We're going to wire you, so you'll be monitored. We won't be far away."

Sam's face was flushed.

"You're going to tell Hog that everything is okay. You've seen the merchandise, and everybody's set to meet on Thursday."

Sam was unconvinced.

"Look, there was some bad blood between me and Hog a while back. He may not trust me. One of our deals went bad."

"Sammy, old buddy, you don't need to worry. The word on the street is that you paid him back, and that he is impressed with you. You're a righteous dude. Besides, you're both from San Berdoo."

Sam nodded languidly. "San Berdoo. Right."

"The only problem you might have with Hog is that he might not like the idea of doing this on Baba Rama's ranch. If he's reluctant,

154

remind him it's the only place the New People's Army will feel safe."

Ford paused and studied me for a moment. "Delano, you just show up at Fernie's tomorrow and tell them when and where the transaction will occur. I'm sure you'll have no trouble."

"Then we're done, right?" I asked.

"No, not quite yet," said Ford. "Sam, you're going to Baba Rama's place with Hog. Eddie, you're going with the New People's Army."

"What for?" I asked. "I thought all we had to do was just help you set it up."

"I told you how it was, Delano. You have to be there Thursday for the exchange. If you guys don't go with them, they'll get suspicious and back out. We've put a lot of time and money into this. Promotions are hanging in the balance here."

"What if we don't do it?"

"If you don't do it, Delano, you'll face a judge Thursday afternoon. For a broken bicycle reflector. And the judge won't like you. I'll make sure of that." His expression softened. "Just be there and play your part. If the leader of the N.P.A. is reluctant, just nudge him along a little. Believe me, he thinks you're some kind of Cuban-trained commando. I don't know what you said to him to give him such an impression, but he thinks you get messages straight from Karl Marx's grave. Any questions?"

"Yeah," I said. "Why does all of this have to happen at Baba Rama's?"

"I told you. Because we want to take him out with the others. He's the biggest dope dealer in this part of the state. Look, I can't tell you everything, but we've got someone on the inside who's already made the arrangement for the transaction to occur at Rama's. You just play it cool."

"If you've got someone on the inside, why do you need us?"

"Because we want it to appear to everyone that you and Sam are setting this up. That way our person will remain above suspicion until it goes down."

"But once everybody is busted, they'll know it was Sam and me that made it happen."

"No. You and Sam will be arrested right along with everyone else. We'll keep all parties separate, and our undercover agent will do the testifying. You and Sam will be off the hook. That's a promise."

On that note, Ford stretched and yawned, and then in mock politeness, he excused himself to leave.

Sam and I sank into the sofa and let the silence speak our fears.

The following morning, Sam received a call and left for the sheriff's department to be wired for the trip to Hog's. Several hours later, I received a similar call and left for Fernie's.

When I arrived, I noticed an unmarked police car parked at the end of the block. The car was plain white and had squad lights visible in the back window. So much for blending in.

I walked into the café and maneuvered my way through a maze of occupied tables and hanging fern plants to the back corner table and sat. I listened to a feminist folk singer complaining about her crappy boyfriends and waited for the N.P.A. to arrive.

Mike and Cheryl entered the café cautiously, like nervous thieves. Mike spotted me first. He tugged at Cheryl's arm and they made their way towards me.

I had not forgotten how pretty Cheryl was. She sat down next to me. I wondered if I should try to warn her before it was too late.

Mike looked around the room suspiciously in all directions, and then he sat down across from me. He leaned forward and looked at me knowingly.

"I knew all along," he said with a smile.

My heart sank to my stomach. I thought my cover was blown before I had said even one word. I fought to keep my composure.

"Knew what, Mike?" asked Cheryl, slightly on edge.

"I knew Eddie was in the movement."

He paused, and I struggled not to show my relief.

"You obviously have had training," he added.

"I'm not at liberty to discuss such matters. All I know is that what you want is waiting for you."

There was a look of awe on his face. His imagination was running wild. I was an agent of intrigue here to assist in his cause.

"Not so fast," said Cheryl. "How do we know this is quality stuff you've got lined up, Delano?"

"Come on," said Mike, turning to Cheryl. "Can't you tell a *comrade* when you're near one?"

"If you don't like what you see," I said, "then don't buy it. This stuff comes right from Fort Ord." I was really winging it now. "You'll see tomorrow. All you have to do is bring the money and meet Hog and his buddies at Baba Rama's ranch."

Mike turned to Cheryl and then back to me. He nodded.

"So it's a deal?" I asked. "We're set for tomorrow morning?"

"Absolutely," said Mike. He reached across the table and shook my hand.

"Then, if that's it, I'll see you here at 8:30. We'll drive up together." With those words I rose from my chair and left the table. I worked my way past the feminist folk singer who was still singing about her crappy boyfriends, around the hanging fern plants and occupied tables, and out the door.

As I walked down the street to my car, a bum sitting on a bench looked up at me from his newspaper and said, "Good job, Delano."

It was Ford. He smirked and tapped an ear plug.

"Just keep walking. See you tomorrow."

I said nothing, walked on to my car, and drove straight home.

That night, long after Alice had gone to sleep, Sam and I sat up talking, drinking coffee, and listening to music. We were still awake but groggy the next morning when Ford nearly knocked down the door. He was wearing black military fatigues and looked pumped up and ready to go.

"You two look like shit!"

Sam and I looked at each other. He looked the way I felt.

"Okay, listen up. You're going to need sunglasses. Do you have sunglasses? Get them. Now. And baseball caps. Jump to it!"

As he walked us outside, Ford instructed us one last time.

"Everything is positioned. Don't panic and everything will be okay. If anything does go wrong, just hit the dirt."

Sam and I looked at each other again. Even with the sunglasses and cap, he still looked like the way I felt.

What a complete fool I was for going along with this. I should be in Mexico right now eating a breakfast burrito.

An unmarked car followed Sam down the road. I'm sure I was followed to Fernie's, where the politicos were waiting for me.

We greeted each other and I went with them to their car. We climbed into the New People's Mercedes. Cheryl drove and Mike sat next to her. I sat alone in the back seat. We left for Baba Rama's.

"You know, Eddie," said Mike turning to me. "This might be small potatoes for a man of your caliber, but once we pull off this library caper, we're going to liberate the park in Pennhill."

"The park? The little park with the swings and seesaw?"

"I know it's not much right now," he said defensively. "But it's just the beginning. We'll call it the New People's Park. It will be something for the working man. After the revolution, the workers are going to need a place to relax."

"I'm glad to see you've been thinking ahead."

He smiled, pleased with himself. Then I saw him look at Cheryl, and *that* look was in his eyes. He was doing this for her, I realized. He wanted to impress her. It was all too familiar to me.

I looked out the window at the passing countryside and thought about all the ridiculous things I'd done to impress women.

After driving up a winding mountain road and crossing a creek, we turned down a dirt road. We meandered our way through a thick grove of redwoods. Soon we approached a gate with a security guard.

My heart stopped. It was the same guy I had accidentally knocked down at the airport. He examined us briefly, but he didn't recognize me, probably because of the sunglasses and baseball cap.

Cheryl drove the Mercedes through the gate. Just ahead, behind a stand of redwoods, were two large buildings. One looked like a dormitory with tiny windows; the other was a warehouse constructed of corrugated tin. On a knoll that rose to one side was a three-story mansion with multiple decks shaded by large trellises.

We parked the car just in front of the house on a wide gravel parking lot. A robed figure approached us, and we were escorted into the house through two large doors and then into Baba Rama's living room. There we were greeted by the fat man himself. He was wearing a yellow muumuu and eating a hot dog for breakfast.

We shook hands, and Baba Rama was especially cordial to Cheryl, holding her hand in his longer than necessary and looking at her warmly.

Cheryl pulled herself away from the fat man.

"Got the C-4?" asked Mike.

"Not so hasty, children," said Baba Rama.

"We didn't come here to socialize," said Cheryl.

"Relax. Soon you will have what you came for." With a delighted gleam in his eye, he added: "Oh, by the way. You did bring the money, didn't you?"

"You'll get the money when we get the C-4," said Mike.

"Yes, I understand," replied the fat man, taking another bite of his hot dog.

Mike leaned close to me and with a cynical smile whispered, "After the revolution, we're going to rid ourselves of vermin like this."

At that moment the loud roar of motorcycle engines distracted us.

"Ah," said Rama. "It is time."

He quickly finished the hot dog and led the way back outside.

There they were, the bikers and a pickup truck. Riding on the back of Hog's bike was Sam, wearing his sunglasses and cap. The guard had not recognized him either.

"More lumpen proletariat," Mike whispered to me. "After Rama, we liquidate these scumbags."

By the time we got to the parking lot, Hog was taking off his gloves and eyeing us suspiciously.

"Where's the stuff?" he asked.

Baba Rama nodded towards the warehouse. Moments later a forklift emerged carrying what must have been bales of marijuana.

Mike went to the trunk of the Mercedes for the money. Hog went to the cab of the pickup truck and retrieved a metal canister.

Everything seemed to be going according to Ford's plan. In one brief moment, it would all be over. All they had to do was to make the physical exchange, and they were just about to do so when I noticed the guard from the gate walking quickly towards us.

Sam looked at me nervously. My anxiety reached a fevered pitch. Then, very simply and quickly, it occurred.

First a briefcase full of money was handed to Baba Rama, then the bales of marijuana were dropped into the truck belonging to Hog, and then the canister of C-4 was passed into Mike's hands.

And then the guard from the gate shouted, "Wait! Cops!"

Cheryl threw me to the ground.

"What the hell..." I cried out, as Sam hit the dirt next to me.

"Shut up," she said, drawing a pistol and a badge. "Del Norte Sheriff's Department! You're all under arrest! Put your hands up!"

Baba Rama threw open his robe and produced a badge and a gun and shouted, "ATF! Put your hands up!"

Hog, stunned by Cheryl and Baba Rama, pulled out a badge and a gun and said, "Freeze! IRS!"

Bewildered, Mike produced a badge and a gun. "Hold on! FBI!"

Suddenly, cops were everywhere. Pandemonium broke out. Who was arresting whom? I was confused. So was Ford.

"Hey, this is our bust!" Ford protested.

"Who the hell are you busting?" shouted Hog.

"You!"

"We're undercover IRS agents! We're here to bust Baba Rama for unreported income."

"I was undercover to bust you and Mike," said Baba Rama, "for possession, transportation and sales of stolen explosives."

"I was here to bust Cheryl for terrorist activities," said Mike.

"I was here to bust all of you!" said Cheryl.

There was a moment or two of silence.

"Is there anybody here who's not in law enforcement?" asked Hog.

"Eddie Delano and Samuel T. Oswald," said Ford, turning to us.

Sam and I stood up.

"Can we bust them for anything?" asked Mike.

"They were helping us bust you," said Ford.

"We're going to look pretty stupid in our reports," said Hog.

"I was up for a promotion," said Mike.

"So was I," said Baba Rama.

"Me too," said Ford.

"And me," said Hog.

Sam and I looked at each other and almost laughed aloud. Then, he said it all, "Look at them. And everyone thinks *I'm* a dumb shit."

"This is what I get for a broken bicycle reflector," I added sarcastically.

Each of them looked at Sam and me with the intent expression of a predator. We looked at each other apprehensively.

"We've got to have something on Eddie Delano," said Mike.

"He's a real threat to national security."

"Well," said Ford. "He does have an outstanding warrant."

"For what?" asked Baba Rama.

"Well," Ford answered timidly. "He failed to appear before a court of law."

"Yeah!" Mike exclaimed triumphantly.

"Eddie didn't do anything," said Sam, coming to my defense. "He got a stupid ticket for a broken bicycle reflector, is all."

They turned their attention to Sam. I saw the wheels turning.

"Sam didn't do anything wrong, either," I said. "You guys set him up on a phony drug bust. Just to get him and me to help you bust each other."

"But we can't end this thing empty-handed," said Baba Rama.

"It's not our fault you screwed up," said Sam.

Slowly, in a state of embarrassed silence, they put their guns and badges away. Then Cheryl turned to us and asked, "You guys need a ride home?"

As we walked with her to a squad car she commandeered from a deputy, we could hear Ford, Hog, Rama, and Mike accusing each other of screwing up a costly investigation.

We got inside the squad car. I sat up front with Cheryl, and Sam took the back seat. As we drove away, I turned to Cheryl and said, "You know, I would never have guessed you for a cop."

"Oh? Why not?"

"Because you're too good-looking."

She looked at me with disgust.

"Pecker for brains," said Sam. "Pecker-for-brains Delano." He looked at me with disappointment and explained, "I suspected her of being a cop from the second I first saw her. She was just too cool."

Cheryl was listening to Sam attentively, and then she looked at me with a snide expression. I turned to Sam.

"All I said was that I would have never figured her for a cop."

"I thought you were supposed to be smarter than me. Maybe if you didn't think with your pecker, you would have known sooner."

Cheryl looked out the window and laughed at the both of us. Then she looked into the mirror at Sam.

"So, what do you do, Sam?"

"I'm an entrepreneur," he answered smoothly. "I wheel and deal in different services and commodities."

"Like what?" she asked with a smile.

"Well, I was a worm farmer for a while."

"Really? My dad farmed worms, among other things."

"My worm farm didn't work out," Sam confessed sadly. "I over-watered those little suckers."

"They don't need a lot of water," she said thoughtfully. "But they need good dirt. You know, there's something my father used to do to the soil." She looked at Sam in the mirror. "If you ever get started up again, I could show you how my father did it."

"Really? I was thinking about starting it up again. I'd appreciate any little bit of help you could give me."

By the time she dropped us off at Sam's place, they had a date for the following night. Needless to say, I was impressed.

That evening as I sat on a lawn chair outside the trailer and watched a beautiful, fiery-red sunset glisten off the bend in the river, I overheard Alice talking to her father on the phone.

"Daddy, if it weren't for Eddie Delano, I'd be in real trouble. He saved me from Baba Rama's evil clutches. He's my hero!" There was a moment of silence. "Yes, Daddy. He's the one I told you about. The war hero who was wounded in Vietnam."

Everything was falling nicely into place. I turned my attention back to the sunset. The furthest thing from my mind just then was whether or not I should get my credential, or whether I should go back to school at all.

The future would take care of itself. The only thing important was being with Alice, and I spent the next few weeks happily at her side.

Then one day I received a letter from Winston:

> *Dear Edward,*
>
> *Think of you often. Ended my brief ca-reer as a Ph.D. candidate: no future in it. Now conducting EST seminars and selling Amway. Easy work. If the M.A. program doesn't work out, think about it. We Hispan-ics have to stick together.*
>
> *Your friend,*
> *W.A.G.*

For a brief moment, I was again filled with doubts, even about Alice. I wondered if I should cut and run out on her before things got too serious.

But she was so damned good-looking. And good to me. In fact, she'd stopped smoking, talking about auras, and hassling me for eating meat. But most importantly, I felt she loved me for who I really was, and I found that especially appealing.

I realized this fully when we were in town one day and ran into a bunch of kids from Herbert Spencer Junior High. Jimmy Crandle was one of them, and he spotted me immediately.

"Delano, we've been looking all over the place for you. You still owe us twenty bucks!"

"Twenty bucks?"

"You promised, and you ain't off the hook! Twenty bucks each!"

"For what?"

"For writing the longest essay!" said Jimmy. "And it was a lot of work, too!"

The others agreed in unison.

"But you couldn't all have written the longest essay," I countered.

Then Alice took my arm. She smiled, reached into her bag, and slipped me five crisp twenty dollar bills. It was the money her father had just sent her.

I paid the kids and they rode away on their bicycles flipping me off. Just before they were out of sight, Jimmy Crandle turned his head and shouted, "Delano, you were the worst fucking teacher we ever had!"

I was about to explain to Alice what had just happened and why, but she stopped me with a kiss. She smiled approvingly, and I realized that I could do no wrong.

We walked on. She didn't say a word.

I was in love.

163

21

Full Circle

So there it was: in spite of the war, drugs, wicked women, and higher education, everything turned out for the best. I had found peace of mind in the mountains with my friends. Sam found worm farming again, and Alice had decided to go back to school.

She was enrolling for the following semester and wanted to major in African drums. We had a mild argument over it when I told her she couldn't major just in drums. But it turned out okay. She went to the music department at the college, and they agreed with me: she couldn't major just in one type of instrument. Her confidence in me was skyrocketing, and with it, my confidence in myself.

Even things with my parents turned out well. They realized that Oscar was a mean-spirited asshole of a dog who deserved to be put to sleep. Last I heard, he had run out of appeals for clemency at the dog pound.

All in all, I was feeling pretty good about myself. I had hurdled difficult challenges that might have crushed a lesser person. I had survived a crazy girlfriend, student-teaching, and my undercover work with the sheriff's department. And I had learned a lot along the way.

But I still couldn't make up my mind about my future. I could start teaching again at Herbert Spencer if I wanted, but I couldn't imagine spending any amount of time at all with that bunch of misfits, let alone eight hours a day for five days a week.

I could go to graduate school, but the only good thing about that would be picking up on young coeds, and I couldn't do that to Alice. I could go into worm farming with Sam, but he was getting most of the help he needed from Cheryl. Besides, I still didn't see the profit in it.

The only thing I was sure of was that I wanted to be with Alice. I thought often about the series of events that had brought us together, and I wondered at my dumb luck.

Then one day while I was helping Sam weed the garden, Winston drove up in a brand-new, red BMW. I was reluctant to see him. I thought he was going to try and sell us Amway stuff or rope us into some kind of EST seminar.

He walked up carrying an expensive briefcase.

"You weren't easy to find, Delano."

"What's up, Winston?" I asked.

"I was just curious about how you were doing."

My bullshit detector was signaling a full red-alert. Winston was not the kind of person to be curious about anything but opportunity.

Sam and I put down our tools and found a comfortable spot on the porch. Winston pulled up an old milk crate and sat with us.

"So, Eddie, how's it going?" he said. "Everybody's talking about the big drug bust fiasco." He smiled sardonically. "I knew immediately you were involved."

He then retrieved from his jacket pocket a little amber bottle and a pocket mirror. Using his briefcase as a flat surface, he placed the mirror on it and poured a white powder onto the mirror. With a credit card, he neatly lined up the white powder. Then he pulled a crisp bill from his wallet, rolled it up into a straw, and offered it to me.

"Want a toot?"

I was mildly curious. I had never tried cocaine before. I started to reach for it, but Sam held back my arm. He shook his head. I had by now learned to trust Sam's instincts about these things.

"No thanks," I said.

Winston snorted the coke and then grinned. He prescribed another line and snorted it, too. Then, beaming with artificial energy, he neatly put everything away.

"So what really brings you up this way?" I asked.

"The truth of the matter," he said, "is that I wanted you to look at my book."

"Your book?" I wasn't entirely sure what he meant.

"Yes, I'm writing about all the clever things I taught you."

He reached into his briefcase and pulled out a bound manuscript and held it up. Across the cover in gold letters was the title, *Waltzing with Mannequins: How to Survive College and Turn a Profit.*

"You say it's about me?" I asked.

"No, it's not just about you, but you *were* my prize pupil, Eddie. If anyone could show how the Winston Ashford Gonzales proven methods work, it'd be you."

In his hands it was impressive. He held it firmly, like a work of fine art. I wondered at how he found the time and inclination to write a book. Maybe he was something more than a simple con artist.

"Look, Eddie," Winston explained. "I'm not going to be on campus any longer. I've moved on to bigger things. But I don't want to let all those things I've taught you go to waste. Besides, I can still make a few bucks from this." He handed it to me with a triumphant smile. "Once it's in print, you can sell it for me at the college."

I opened it. On the first page was the title again, and under it, Winston's name. I began to thumb through it. Page two was blank. I turned to page three, and it was also blank. So were pages four and five. I thumbed through the entire manuscript, and all of the pages were blank!

"Are you sure you gave me the right book? There's nothing here."

"That's the right book," he replied with a confident smile.

"This isn't a book. There's just a title page with your name on it. All the other pages are blank!"

"I was hoping you could fill in the rest."

Sam and I looked at each other and laughed. Winston was so full of himself that he didn't realize we were laughing at him. He continued on as if I'd already agreed to write his manuscript.

"I figure you'll knock it out in a couple of weeks," he said.

"Why would I want to write a book for you?"

"You wouldn't be writing it yourself. I'd be monitoring you closely. I'd tell you what I had in mind, and you'd put some flesh on the bone, so to speak."

"That's a lot of work." I was too bewildered to think of anything better to say.

"I know what you're angling for," he said coyly. "You want to know what's in it for you. That's what I always liked about you, Eddie." He paused. "I'll take care of you. I'll give you something for your trouble."

"Like what?"

"When the book is ready to sell, I'll give you sole distributorship of my work at Del Norte. Of course, that means you'll only get a small percentage of the take. But if you play it smart, you can build a pyramid through your distribution. In no time, you'll have people under you, selling my book to others, and you'll collect a percentage of their profits. You'll make a lot of money. I guarantee it!"

I looked at him in stunned silence.

"Well, I can't really guarantee anything," he added. "Your success is up to you. If you're motivated and have a positive attitude, you can accomplish anything."

"A distributorship? It hardly seems worthwhile."

"Well," he said excitedly. "What if I sweeten the offer? I'll give you fifty bucks up front."

I was again stunned into silence. I looked at Sam, and he had caution written all over his face.

"Okay, make it seventy-five. But that's as high as I can go."

"Winston, that's a lot of work for seventy-five bucks."

"It couldn't be that much work. I have such good ideas, and we've already put them to the test. All you have to do is turn them into a book."

"Then why don't you do it?"

"Well, I just don't have a lot of time on my hands right now. Anyway, I kind of figured you owed it to me."

"What do you figure I owe you?"

"Eddie, without me you would be nothing. Seventy-five bucks is a generous offer."

He was smacking his lips, and his eyes were twitching. I wasn't sure whether or not he was conscious of the fact that he was conning me. It was, after all, second nature to him.

"Besides," he said, "I'd be immortalizing you by putting you in my book."

"It's not a book, Winston. At best, it would be a study guide. That is, if anyone ever agrees to write it for you."

"Okay, it's a study guide. Call it what you want. It's going to generate a lot of money."

"I'm really not interested."

"Okay, I'll make the entire book about you, if you agree to write it. After all, we Hispanics have to stick together."

Sam interjected, "So, will there be anything in that book about me?"

"Yes. As a matter of fact, I intend to mention you, Sam. Of course, I won't use your real name."

"What are you going to say about me?" he asked.

"You're Delano's primitive roommate. He uses you for an anthropology project proving the missing link theory."

Sam's face turned red. I watched him shake his head in disgust and walk away from us.

I turned back to Winston and whispered angrily, "You didn't have to say that!"

He looked puzzled at my comment. I realized, for the first time, the depth of his limitations. I took a deep breath and tried a different tack.

"I can't write it, Winston," I said matter-of-factly. "It's against my principles. I came here to avoid work, remember?"

I returned the manuscript to him.

"I can see you need some time to think about it."

"Haven't you heard even one word I've just said? I made up my mind five minutes ago. Winston, I'm not writing a book for you. That's a lot of work, and the best you can do is offer me seventy-five bucks! Do you think I'm that stupid?"

"Of course not." He paused for a moment, considering. "You drive a hard bargain, Delano. Okay. One hundred bucks now, one hundred when you're finished, and three percent of the profit once you start selling it!"

"No, no, no. You want a book, you write it yourself!"

"Okay, Eddie. I can see that I've overestimated you. I really thought you'd want to take responsibility for your life, but I can see that you'd rather end up some poor loser than become the sole proprietor of a Winston Ashford Gonzales distributorship."

"You want me to write *your* book for you, and you're telling me about *responsibility?*"

Sam returned and angrily told Winston, "It's about time for you to make yourself scarce. Good bye!"

Winston was startled. He looked to me for support. I nodded my head in agreement with Sam.

"Well, Eddie. I guess I'm no longer welcome here." Winston was offended, but it was not his nature to show it. He retrieved a business card from his wallet and handed it to me. "Give me a call when you've given it more thought."

I took the card. Winston smiled and held out his hand.

"No hard feelings, Eddie."

Reluctantly, I returned the handshake, deliberately withholding any enthusiasm. He walked away from the porch, got into his red car, and left in a trail of dust.

For a day or two, Winston's visit was a topic of conversation. Sam was adamant that Winston was not a good influence.

"I get bad vibrations from him, Eddie. Always have."

Moreover, Sam was appalled that Winston had tried to get me to write a book. He reminded me of his friend who he was sure had got a brain tumor from reading too many books. He warned me of the incalculable consequences of *writing* one.

Alice agreed with Sam's assessment of Winston's character, but she thought the idea of writing a book was a good one.

"I've always thought you were a good writer," she said.

She told me I could use it as credit towards a master's degree. I found that hard to believe, and we had a mild argument over it. But, as it turned out, she was right. I could write a creative piece in lieu of a master's thesis.

I considered the possibilities. I had written enough papers, both before and after I met Winston, to know that writing was not easy. But it had to be easier than facing those deluded clowns and juvenile delinquents at Herbert Spencer Junior High on a daily basis. Hell, I'd farm worms before I did that.

Although I wasn't at all sure about the master's degree, the idea of writing a book began to take hold. Whenever I had actually written about a subject in the past, I had indeed learned something. Writing a book about my experiences might help me sort things out. And that was important to me.

In fact, the more I thought about it, the more I realized that I had done Winston a favor. If he did actually write his own book, it might make an honest man of him. Maybe that was just what he needed. Maybe that was what we all needed.

I awoke from a deep and restful sleep to the aroma of fresh-brewed coffee. Alice's eyes lit up when she saw I was awake, and she smiled with a faint blush.

"I'm going out to the garden to pick breakfast."

I got up and poured myself a cup of coffee. On the small kitchen table were a catalogue of classes, Alice's music books, and a new yellow tablet.

I pulled the yellow tablet out from under the pile and pushed the other books aside. Alice had doodled on it. In neat schoolgirl penmanship she'd written, "Eddie loves Alice!" She had surrounded the words with cute little flowers and hearts.

I looked out the window and watched her move about the garden. She was picking tomatoes. She wore an old straw hat, a faded red tee shirt, and Levi's which were frayed at the knees. I thought again about my good fortune. I was really lucky to be with her.

I picked up a pen and turned to a clean page of the tablet.

You might think I'm stupid for shooting off my big toe, but at the time it seemed like a good idea.